BEYOND FOREVER

ONCE UPON A BRIDESMAID (BOOK 2)

ELLE WRIGHT

Beyond Forever
Once upon a Bridesmaid, Book Two

———

Elle Wright

Beyond Forever
Copyright © 2017 by Elle Wright

Excerpt from *It's Always Been You* copyright © 2017 by Elle Wright
Excerpt from *The Forbidden Man* copyright © 2015 by Elle Wright

ISBN: 978-0-9994213-0-7
1st Edition

Elle Writes Books Publishing
Ypsilanti, Michigan
www.ellewright.com

Editor:
Latoya C. Smith, LCS Literary Services

Proofreading:
Christine Hughes,

Cover Design:
Sherelle Green

❀ Created with Vellum

Ryleigh Fields has plans for her life that don't involve weddings, marriage, or true love. Returning to her hometown is hard, but her agenda is clear: drink, eat, and leave as fast as she can. In that order. But when she stupidly agrees to a wedding pact with her besties and promptly runs into the one guy who could be a game changer, Ryleigh realizes that even the best laid plans can be derailed.

Martin Sullivan travels all over the world for Marshall and Sullivan Consulting. Each destination offers exposure for his software company, more money in his pocket, and a bevy of attractive women. But a trip to his cousin's wedding, puts him in direct contact with the one woman he can't stop thinking about.

After consulting on a project, Martin knew he'd met his match with Ryleigh. One perfect night in Brazil, and he was ready to let her know just how much she impressed him, but he never got the opportunity. Now, almost a year later, he has his chance. The problem? Convincing Ryleigh. And like always, he's up for the challenge.

To my mother, Regina, you are missed. Love you forever.

ACKNOWLEDGMENTS

Beyond Forever was a labor of love. I had so much fun writing it, but the best part was collaborating with the amazing Sherelle Green, Sheryl Lister, and Angela Seals. I also can't thank Latoya C. Smith and Christine Hughes enough for sticking with me. It was truly an awesome experience. Thank you so much for listening to the "crazy" idea and stepping out there with me. I'm looking forward to Once Upon A…

There are so many people to thank, I'm sure I'll forget someone. But first and foremost, I want to thank God. I am nothing without Him. It is because of Him that I have this gift, that I have this imagination. He made me, after all. I'm so grateful.

In 1991, I met this amazing man. Well, he was a boy at the time. There was something about him that immediately drew me to him. I had to get to know him. From there, we became friends. Then, I realized that my life wouldn't work without him.

To my *one*… Now, after 18 years of marriage, I know my life is better because of you, Jason. I love you. Thank you for your unwavering support.

To my children, thank you for being my inspiration. You are the air I breathe, the wind in my sails. Love you all!

To my family and friends, I love you all. You know who you are.

I also want to thank the many bloggers, reviewers, and book clubs that have supported me from day one. I could not have done this without you. Thank you for encouraging me through your thoughtful reviews, messages, and chats. I appreciate you.

Thank you to my fellow authors in the romance community. We are all winning! I want to give a special shout out to the "City Chicks and Southern Belles." It was an honor to be included at an event that featured all of you. You all ROCK!

For everyone reading *Beyond Forever*, I hope you enjoy the slice of humor and heat Ryleigh and Martin bring. Thank you for taking a chance on me. I am so appreciative.

THE PACT

Wedding schedule, wedding colors, wedding programs, wedding pictures, wedding toast number 5,789, wedding blah, wedding shit... If Ryleigh Fields heard the "W" word one more time, she was liable to choke someone—namely her BFF Ava Prescott for putting her in this situation in the first place.

It wasn't like she wouldn't walk on hot, molten rocks with her bare feet for Ava. She would do that and more for her besties, Ava, Mackenzie Cannon, Raven Holloway, and Quinn Jacobs. It wasn't even that she'd been forced to wear a two-hundred-plus-dollar chiffon, floor-length dress that she'd never wear again. In fact, she was pretty sure the dress would be in the trash before she left the reception hall. *Who wears pewter anything?* No. It was simple. Weddings made everyone go bat-shit crazy. Like abso-fuckin'-lutely insane.

Ryleigh was over-the-moon happy for her friend, Ava. Really. She'd even admit to shedding a tear when the happy couple exchanged those heartfelt, handwritten vows. But between the wedding planner sending multiple emails a day and barking orders about folding programs and walking in a straight line, Mrs. Prescott nitpicking about centerpieces and menu choices, and Ava crying at the drop of a hat about Lord knows what, Ryleigh was fed up. She mistakenly thought she was home free after the ceremony, but the wedding planner from hell still wouldn't leave her alone. And she hoped—no, she seriously prayed—that she could get out of town without going the fuck off on the next person that asked her when she was going to be next. Because this shit was getting on her fucking nerves.

Ryleigh turned her attention to her friend Quinn, who was standing before them with a smile as wide as that damn fat cat in Cinderella. Ryleigh wanted to make an excuse to leave because Quinn had been waxing poetic since Ava announced her engagement months ago, and she just wasn't in the mood for fairy tales. Her life was anything but, and one man with a cute smile and a magic penis wouldn't change her mind. Sure, she knew Q was the hopeless, poetic romantic in their crew. She didn't begrudge that because that optimism had gotten her through the worst times of her life. But damn... She was tired and pretty sure her hair looked a hot mess because of all the manual labor she'd been forced to do. She was so sick of this freaking wedding.

Sighing, Ryleigh rolled her eyes and twisted in her chair to face Mac and Raven. "Can we just tell her to shut up now?" she mumbled under her breath. "The wedding is over, and my drink is gone. Ouch." Ryleigh rubbed her leg where Raven had pinched her.

Despite the sting that radiated in the spot, she couldn't help but smile at Raven. She'd missed them. These women weren't just her friends, they were her family. The only family she had. Growing up in the tight-knit community of Rosewood Heights, South Carolina had presented many challenges for Ryleigh. The town was too tiny for her taste, especially since she'd been the black sheep of their group of friends. Always the charity case, Ryleigh had come to hate their small-as-hell town. The whispers about her crazy mother and absent father hadn't abated in the eleven years since she'd left for college in Michigan. She'd endured the sympathetic smiles of the old church ladies who pretended to want to help her but gossiped about behind her back. The kids on the playground had teased her mercilessly about her lack of fashionable clothes, but she'd dealt with it. Ryleigh had known early on that Rosewood Heights was not her endgame and she worked damn hard to be self-sufficient enough to make sure she'd never have to darken her mother's doorstep, begging to come home, like Harriet Fields swore she would.

"Ha!" Mac's voice brought her out of her reluctant trip down Rosewood Heights Memory Lane starring everything-that-was-wrong-with-this-damn-town. "Anyone within a thirty-mile radius can hear her squeal when she starts talking about love and shit."

Ryleigh didn't know what had transpired before that point, but she could agree with Mac's statement. She gave Mac a high-five. "Girl, you can say that again."

"If everyone's done making fun of me, can we please continue this discussion?" Quinn said, clearing her throat.

Shit. Ryleigh scanned the area for anyone that she could convince to bring her another margarita—with a double shot of Patron preferably.

Kicking off the four-inch strappy sandals Ava required they rock, she slouched back in the wicker chair.

Raven leaned over to her. "Don't look now, but you have an admirer."

"If it's not Idris, I don't care. Where is that damn waiter?"

As if on cue, the young waiter appeared before her with fresh drinks. *Yes.* She snatched her top-shelf margarita off the tray, winking at the cutie pie. *Too bad he's one foot out of jail bait.*

"I think we should toast." Quinn held up a shaky glass full of margarita that Ryleigh knew she wasn't going to finish. *I'll finish that one, too.* "Here's to us all finding that special one and saying 'I do' this time next year."

What the...? Slamming her glass down on the table, Ryleigh resisted the urge to bolt. "Oh hell no."

She vaguely heard Raven say something next to her, then Mac, but she couldn't recall what it was because she was too busy wondering what the hell was wrong with Quinn. They all knew she was itching to follow in Ava's footsteps down the aisle, but how did that equate to all of them trotting their asses to the altar, too.

Quinn continued, but Ryleigh had effectively blocked her out. No way. No fucking way. She was going home. It was time to get off this train before it was too late. She turned to Raven, who'd apparently lost her damn mind, too, because she was raising her glass in agreement. Then, she looked up at Quinn. It was the hopeful look in Q's eyes that did her in every single time. And her hopeful friend had just issued a "Best Friend's Challenge." And she'd never backed down from one, in all their years of friendship. No matter how crazy they were. And this was crazy as hell. She wasn't even dating, or trying to be anyone's girlfriend. She had plans for her life; ones that didn't involve becoming a wife.

Okay, so she could agree to this right now and then not get married. Simple. It wasn't like there was money or a promotion on the line. They weren't in a damn Lifetime movie. After a year, she wouldn't be married, and that was all to it. Losing the challenge wouldn't be the end of the world. She was grown ass woman. She'd lost before, sometimes on purpose.

What could they do anyway? Fire her from being their best friend because she didn't find and marry some man in one year. *Who does that anyway*? Shit, Ava and Owen had been dating for years before he'd proposed. It was a harmless, hopeful toast that would make her friend feel better. She could do that.

Slowly, she raised her glass as Mac and Quinn went back and forth about something.

Finally, Mac raised her glass and Quinn said, "To finding that special one and saying 'I do' by this time next year."

The four friends clinked their glasses, and Ryleigh gulped down the rest of her drink. It wasn't nearly enough to get the sour taste of that toast out of her head. With that in mind, and without another word, she stood and made a beeline for the bar.

1

R yleigh zoomed through the massive ballroom, toward the bar in the corner. The smile plastered on her face served as a barrier to people who'd tried to stop her on her way. The meaningless small talk she'd heard throughout the evening was wearing on her. *Ryleigh, you look gorgeous. Ryleigh, I hear you're doing well for yourself. Wow, Ryleigh, we missed you around town.* And her favorite... *Ryleigh, your turn next*?

"Bartender, I'd like a Margarita, heavy on the Patron." Ryleigh tapped the bar counter. "Never mind, just make it a double shot, hold the Margarita mix."

A few minutes later, the bartender set a shot on the bar and smiled. She grinned and dropped a tip into the glass vase in front of him.

"Ryleigh."

She froze, recognizing the voice immediately, even from across the room. Narvin Long? *This is a nightmare.* "I'm pretty sure this isn't your normal protocol," she said to the confused bartender. "But, can you hold my drink while I hide?"

Not waiting for an answer, she shuffled around the corner and into the ladies restroom. Once glance in the mirror and she rolled her eyes. It was just as she thought—her hair was a hot ass mess. She ran her fingers through her short curls and smoothed a hand down the back. Pulling her cellphone from the pocket of her dress, she browsed her social media pages for a few minutes.

Finally, she pushed the door open and poked her head out. When she saw no sign of Narvin, she stepped out. As she turned the corner, she spotted Narvin lurking at the bar. She stopped in her tracks and waited, with her back against the wall.

Narvin? Well, he just happened to be her "first." The clumsy, awkward, one-minute induction into the sexed-up club was one of her many regrets. Not because Narvin wasn't nice. He had been the ultimate gentleman; had taken her out for a burger and fries at the Sonic Drive-In before he de-virginized her. Ryleigh had been the first to lose her virginity among her friends, technically winning that Best Friend's Challenge. Unfortunately, the experience was pretty forgettable and she'd been forced to avoid him for the rest of high school. It was so bad, she didn't even tell her friends that she'd won, and ultimately had let Mac take the prize.

Ole' Narvin hadn't deserved her cold shoulder then, and he definitely didn't now. But she couldn't bring herself to face him. What exactly would she say? *I'm sorry I ignored you for all these years*? What if he asked why? What if he asked her out? Could she tell him that the smell of cheese and ground beef on his breath had scarred her for life and caused an aversion to Sonic that she'd never quite been able to shake? That sex with him wasn't what she thought it'd be? A simple "Hi" would not be enough for this situation that's why it was better that she just avoided him.

"Sir, can you tell me where the woman who was just standing here went?" she heard Narvin asked the bartender.

Ryleigh giggled at the frazzled explanation the bartender gave, biting down on her fist. Obviously, lying wasn't his strong suit. If she hadn't seen him eyeing one of the groomsmen like a steak dinner, she might have hit on him.

After a few, long minutes, she peeked around the corner. Coast was clear. Smoothing a hand down her dress, she started back toward the bar and… *Shit.*

Ryleigh dropped her head and turned away as the town whore-monger Miles Henderson breezed past her, leaving his cheap cologne in his wake. The last thing she needed was to run into that jerk. The cocky bastard would more than likely talk her ears off before he propositioned her. It wouldn't be the first or last time she'd turned him down, especially after his disappointing perfor-mance in high school.

This freaking town is as small as the girdle I've been choking in all day.

Ava rounded the corner, stopping when she spotted her. "Ry, where have you been?" Her friend glanced around their imme-diate area, a confused expression on her flawless face. "Why are facing the wall with your head down? Are you hiding?"

Ryleigh swallowed. "Did you have to invite every guy I've had sex with to your wedding?"

Ava laughed. "Girl, you better stop."

Ryleigh couldn't help but smile. "I'm so serious, Ava." She relaxed then, and looked at her best friend.

Ava was stunning, a vision in white. Ryleigh had always believed her friend to be one of the prettiest women she'd ever met face to face, but Ava in all her wedding glory was beautiful. They'd come a long way from the girls who'd played with Barbie in the attic all those years ago.

"I'm so glad you're here." Ava hooked an arm in hers. "I've missed you."

Ava was the only one in their group of five that had stayed behind in Rosewood Heights. The Prescott family was the wealth-iest family in town, and pretty much owned everything. Yet, they weren't pretentious. They were warm and supportive, a surrogate family for her. Growing up, Ryleigh didn't have much. She was the only child, the result of a toxic relationship between two people that should have never been parents. Her mother was pretty much absent, lost in the haze of her addiction and her men. And her father? Well, he was an ass who'd deserted her when she'd needed him the most. Ryleigh had to fend for herself for much of her life.

The Prescott's had taken her under their wing, inviting her on summer and winter vacations. When she graduated from high school, it was Mr. Prescott that wrote a check for Ryleigh's college tuition. She could never repay them for their generosity. Staying in the sprawling Prescott Manor on the north side of town was her safe haven. That house symbolized hope, not because of its size, but because of the people in it.

"I wish you'd come visit more often," Ava continued.

"It's hard," Ryleigh admitted. Every time she'd come home, there was some sort of drama. Her mother was ornery and manipulative, and made her visits hell. This trip was no exception. After her mother had shown up drunk to the ceremony, Ryleigh had to give her mother a couple hundred bucks to get her to leave without causing a scene.

Ava nodded. "I know. But this is your home, too."

Tears threatened to fall, but Ryleigh willed them away. "I'm here now, Ava. I'm so happy for you and Owen."

Owen Sullivan was what they'd call "new money" in these parts. His family wasn't born wealthy, but they'd earned it the old-fashioned way. Hard work. Ryleigh couldn't help but respect it. After all, that's what she intended to do. Shit, she was already on her way.

"Are you ready for the big night?" Ryleigh asked, with a wink.

Ryleigh didn't know how she'd done it, but Ava had managed to wait until this day to lose her virginity. It was a feat considering Owen was like sex on a stick with his chocolate skin and lean frame. They'd all teased her about it over the years, but Ava had held true to her vow of celibacy until marriage.

Hell, next to Ava, Ryleigh felt like a heathen. Narvin and Miles aside, she'd never been shy about sex. She loved wrapping herself around a man, even if only for a night...or two.

"I'm ready." Ava smiled wistfully. "And thank you for the pointers. I think he'll enjoy what I have for him."

Ryleigh bumped her hip into Ava's. "Just don't choke, girlfriend."

They both burst out in laughter. Oh, she'd definitely missed laughing with the women who knew her better than anyone. Yes, they'd texted each other regularly, talked on the phone often, and there was their monthly kick-in-the-butt conference call. Those things were all well and good, but to be able to actually lay eyes on her "girls" was everything.

"I love you, Ava. You deserve all the happiness you can stand."

The two embraced in a tight hug. After tomorrow, Ryleigh would be back at home in Detroit, away from her family again. With a heavy heart, she pulled away from her best friend, her sister.

Ava brushed a tear from her cheek. "Love you, too, Ry."

"I need a drink. Did you know this girdle had my boobs all up in my chin? I've been tempted to cut this mug off all night."

They giggled before Owen strolled over to them and pulled Ava away to meet a great-aunt of his. Before she went, though, Ava turned and blew a kiss at Ryleigh. Ryleigh reciprocated with a cheeky grin. It was an Ava and Ryleigh thing that had started for some reason right around the age of five. She couldn't remember why, but it had stuck through the years.

After she lost sight of her friend and her new husband, Ryleigh glanced back at the bar. The music was blaring, the drinks were flowing, and Ryleigh was suddenly feeling like she couldn't breathe. She stalked back over to the bartender, who immediately set her shot glass back on the bar.

"Thanks," she said, taking the shot in one gulp. "Another."

Time to do what she'd set out to do. Drink tequila, party with her friends, go to sleep, and get the hell out of Rosewood Heights. In that order. When the bartender slid her another full shot, she reached out to take it.

"Finally, I get you alone." The low timbre was hot in her ear, warming her from her toes to her ears. *It couldn't be.*

Words escaped her as she waited for more words, for more

anything. Her heart hammered in her chest as the seconds ticked by. The last time she'd heard *that* voice, seen *that* face, had been in Brazil.

"I've been watching you all day, wondering if you taste as good as I remember, if you'll still whimper when I touch you here."

He brushed his finger against the sensitive area behind her ear and she bit back a groan.

"You walked out on me, Ryleigh Fields. And you stole something of mine. I want it back." She felt his nose against her ear, his lips over her jaw. "No words?"

"Martin," she breathed.

He snatched up her shot glass and, seconds later, set the empty glass back down on the bar. The intoxicating smell of tequila mixed with the spicy, male scent of him washed over Ryleigh and her eyes drifted closed.

"That's my name." His strong hands gripped her hips. "Turn around."

Ryleigh was a formidable woman, in and out of the bedroom. But the low command in his voice made her quiver on her bare feet. Because, yes. She'd been walking around without shoes for the past half an hour.

Taking a steadying breath, she turned slowly. But she didn't dare look up because she knew what she'd see. His was an understated beauty. Visibly, he was attractive. But it wasn't what drew her to him. It was his dry wit, his beautiful mind, his strong hands, that disarming smile, his smooth brown skin, and those *fuck-me* hazel eyes. Martin Sullivan could definitely get it. And he had. Which was exactly the problem.

Wait. *Martin Sullivan?*

Her eyes flashed to his, and she almost forgot that she needed air to live. Steeling herself, she let out a slow breath and cursed her body for responding to the nearness of him. "You're related to Owen." It wasn't a question. "That's why you're here."

The corner of his mouth quirked up, and she wondered if he could tell she was melting. "Imagine my surprise..." He traced a finger down her chin and neck to the "V" in her dress. "And my glee when I saw you walking down the aisle."

She smacked his finger away. "Don't do that."

"Why, doll?"

"Don't call me that."

"I couldn't keep my eyes off of you." His gaze was like a soft caress, like he was actually touching her with his talented fingers.

"Martin, you can't do this. You can't be here."

He cradled her face in his hands, sweeping his thumbs over her ear lobes. "But I am here. And I'd say it's fate."

"This is my family, my friends. I have to go. I'm a bridesmaid. I have bridesmaid duties."

"So that's why you're here knocking back shots and hiding from random men?"

Oh God. "You saw that, huh?"

"Don't worry, though. I'll keep your secret if you keep mine."

Curiosity had her leaning forward, practically arching into him to hear his secret. "What?" she whispered.

He bent lower, blew in her ear, then sucked the sensitive lobe into his mouth. Ryleigh sucked in a haggard breath and held on to his arms for dear life.

"You want to hear my secret, doll?"

"Yes." She hadn't meant for her voice to sound all needy and breathy, but Martin seemed to have that effect on her. Everything about him was trouble. On paper, he was a mother's dream for her daughter: successful entrepreneur and a smart businessman, degrees from University of Michigan and Duke University. But the way he made her feel, reckless and free, beautiful and sexy—that wasn't good. Because those qualities would not get her to where she wanted to be, where she needed to be. And she would be damned if she ended up like her mother. All that potential thrown away for a man that wasn't worth the last $5 bill her mother used to pay for her father's bus ticket out of town. She'd watched her mother drown her sorrows at the bottom of a bottle and swore she'd never let a man control her emotions like that. As good, as fine, and as hot as Martin Sullivan was, Ryleigh Fields was not the one.

Before she could form the words in her head and say what needed to be said, his lips met hers. His arm wrapped around her waist, pulling her soft body against his hard one. And she was lost.

MARTIN SULLIVAN HAD MADE a living fixing shit. He was sought after by companies on the brink of ruin due to their outdated information systems. He didn't take orders, he made moves. His competitors never saw him coming until he was miles away with their clients. No, he wasn't cocky, just confident in his abilities—in and out of the boardroom. That's why he was hard-pressed to find a reason for his current predicament.

Martin wished he could say that his bruised ego had propelled him to boldly proposition Ryleigh Fields in the middle of his cousin's wedding reception, everybody else be damned. After all, this woman had been the only woman that had ever left in the middle of the night without so much as a goodbye, asshole. She'd disappeared like a puff of smoke before he could ask for her personal phone number, before he could articulate how much he'd enjoyed himself in her arms. They'd spent what he had thought was one of the best nights of his adult life in his rented villa in Brazil, making love until he'd passed out from exhaustion. There were no texts, no emails...nothing. Instead, he was left wanting her, thinking about her every single day for the last six months.

But he couldn't concentrate on the excuses when her mouth was pressed against his, when she'd opened to him so willingly, when she moaned low in her throat as his hands swept up her back and pulled her even closer, when her tongue was teasing his own, when her teeth were...biting him? He reared back, muttering a string of curses. *Damn.*

When he glared at her, he noticed the gleam in her gorgeous

brown eyes. *Challenge accepted.* "You bit me." He let out a humor-less chuckle before he ran a thumb over his bottom lip.

"You kissed me." She propped a hand on her hip, and he caught the way she swayed slightly.

Martin couldn't help but smirk. He was absolutely sure of his ability to read people. It had gotten him very far in life. His grand-mother had called it a gift, and he embraced it. Ryleigh wanted him. He'd known it from the first day he'd laid eyes on her. He'd read it in her like he was studying for the hardest exam of his life. But her walls were as thick and as high as the Great Wall of fucking China.

"Okay, that's fair." He inched closer to her, and she didn't back away. He'd expect nothing less from the beautiful spitfire in front of him. Honestly, he hadn't planned to kiss her. In fact, his only goal was to disarm her so much with his presence that she would agree to sit down with him and have a drink. "I shouldn't have kissed you without an invitation."

"Exactly."

"I didn't know you knew Ava." He figured a change of subject would help alleviate the tension in the air.

"I've known her for years. She's one of my dearest friends. You're Owen's…?"

"Cousin. Our fathers are brothers."

"Yeah?" She crossed her arms over her breasts and he had to resist the urge to pull her back to him so he could feel her against his body. It had been a long time, and he could admit that being near her fired up every nerve ending in his body. She smelled like fresh rain and flowers. "What a small world. Are you and Owen close?"

He hummed as if he had to think about it, enjoying the way she gripped the column of her throat. "We used to be, until high school. My parents moved away from our hometown."

"I know the feeling. Ava is the only one that stayed in Rose-wood Heights after we graduated."

The polite conversation grated on his nerves, but he would

rather her talk about the weather than walk away. "So, tell me about Rin and Tin."

Her eyebrows drew together. "Who?"

"The two men you were hiding from. Rin and Tin?"

She laughed then, and he found himself leaning forward even more. "You're crazy." She waved him off. "They are nobodies, just some guys I went to school with. Hometown boys."

"You looked like you would do anything to get away from them."

Shrugging, she said, "Hey, you know as well as I do that some people are best left in the past."

He chuckled, remembering a conversation they'd had over drinks one warm night in Brazil. He'd admitted that it was hard for him to go back to old relationships and old situations because the past was indeed the past. Funny how that conversation had come back to bite him in the… lip. Because Ryleigh was anything but a past that he wanted to run from.

Martin reached out and pushed the strap of her dress up, taking a chance by grazing her shoulder with his knuckle.

Her plump lips parted. "You really should watch yourself. How do you know I don't have a man? It's very presumptuous of you to come waltzing in here and act like you own me."

He snickered. "Boyfriend?" The thought made him want to punch someone. "Damn, just when I was hoping you'd join me for a drink and a little fuck for old time's sake." When she opened her mouth, he rushed on, "Just kidding. Ryleigh, I think we're beyond games, don't you?"

Her gaze dropped to the floor.

"We used to be cool. I see no reason why we can't be friends. I'm in town for the next few days. I've never been here. How about you show me around?"

Although most of their time together had consisted of work-related dinners, drinks with the team after a long day of testing, and countless meetings, Martin had been well aware of the sexual chemistry between them. It was an instant attraction, hard to ignore, but impossible to explore. Ryleigh was a colleague, and any relationship between them was dangerous for his company.

Martin had figured out early on that Ryleigh wasn't easy to get to know. But eventually, they'd bonded over their mutual love of art, and had managed to carve out a sort of friendship.

Ryleigh met his gaze. "Okay, I'm staying at Prescott Manor. We can meet for breakfast in the morning. But don't get any ideas. There will be no repeat of Brazil."

"I promise. I won't even touch you. I'll be on my best behavior." Leaning in closer, he whispered against her ear, "You can breathe now."

Ryleigh relaxed a little, her shoulders dropping on a soft sigh. "Marty Mar, you play too much."

He raised his hands in surrender. "Oh, that's low. You know how much I hate that."

As a child, he'd grown sick of the Martin Lawrence jokes. Everything from the high-octave "What's Up?" to "Can I roll with you?" to "Get ta steppin'!" It seemed like everyone always had something to say when they found out his name. It was corny as hell, and he'd made it known at some point down in Brazil. Of course, that had only made the team do it more.

She giggled and he smiled at the light in her eyes. "I'm sorry. That was low. I have to go. Enjoy the rest of your evening."

"Oh. Before you go, that doesn't mean the offer isn't still on the table. I want you, and you know it. I just won't touch you until you beg for it."

Ryleigh turned on her heels and bolted toward a table of ladies. Martin knew he was wrong, so damn wrong. But there was no way in hell he was leaving Rosewood Heights without getting a taste of Ms. Ryleigh Fields.

2

Martin nursed his cognac and observed the festivities around him. The wedding reception was still in full swing. The drinks were flowing and Ryleigh was still there. She hadn't bolted like he'd halfway expected, wedding party be damned. His parents had made their way back to their hotel, but his cousins were just getting started on the dance floor.

After the spectacle he'd made earlier, kissing Ryleigh as if the entire Sullivan clan wasn't watching, had made him the topic of discussion. Normally, it would have bothered him but he could care less what they thought. He wanted Ryleigh. That fact hadn't changed. Ever.

When his company, Marshall and Sullivan, landed the coveted account with a major automotive company in the Detroit area, he'd jumped at the chance to dig in. Unlike similar companies, he and his partner, Carter, had made it a point to be involved in a project from day one. Martin liked to get his hands dirty in the details of a project, often cozying up to the "little" people of an organization. He preferred to get input from the people actually doing the job.

That's how he'd found himself in Brazil. Ryleigh's employer

had been launching a new vehicle, and she was the project manager. Martin still remembered the day he'd met her. She'd incorrectly assumed he was simply an employee of the firm, and he'd never bothered to correct her assumption.

Thinking back, he wasn't sure if his deception had been a test for her or him. Several weeks had passed before he shared his true role in the company with her. His admission hadn't changed how she interacted with him. Most women he'd run across quickly changed their tune when they found out that he actually owned a multi-million-dollar company. But Ryleigh wasn't a normal woman. Admittedly, he'd been even more intrigued by her. Martin had never wanted to know someone like he'd wanted to know Ryleigh then. He'd watched her, noted the way she worked, how her subordinates responded to her. What he'd found was Ryleigh treated everyone—from the janitors to senior management —the same.

Initially, his plan was to go down to Brazil, set things up, and switch off with one of his lead employees. Once his time was up, he'd realized he couldn't leave. And he knew it was only because of her.

After the launch, on his last night in Brazil, he'd invited Ryleigh out for drinks. Spending time with her outside of the work crew had been a special treat for him. She was a breath of fresh air; genuine, funny, and intelligent. They'd bonded over sports and food. She was perfect. Before he could help himself, he'd invited her to his villa for drinks. They'd talked for hours about nothing and everything, and when he'd asked her to stay, she did. All night.

Shaking his mind of the hot memories, Martin sipped his drink. He caught sight of Ryleigh on the dance floor, twerking with her friends. Her sun-kissed skin was glowing. The braids she wore in Brazil had been replaced with a short cut that exposed the delicate column of her neck that he knew she loved him to touch. Ryleigh was thick, with full hips and long legs that he wanted wrapped around him. Everything about her made him feel a little crazy with need for her.

He loved the easy way she interacted with those around her, and noted that many people seemed sincerely fond of her. He'd witnessed countless hugs and kisses from wedding guests as they passed her by. Her smile, accentuated with those deep dimples, caught the attention of more than a few men in the room. Yes, he'd noticed. It made him want to brand her, then drag her to his hotel room and make love to her all night.

Smirking, he rubbed a hand over his bottom lip. That bite was a small price to pay for the opportunity to hold her in his arms again. As if she'd been reading his mind, she glanced over at him from the far side of the dance floor. Their eyes held for a moment before she turned her attention to one of her friends.

It wouldn't be long now. Martin knew it was only a matter of time before she'd come to him. She couldn't deny the pull any more than he could. Then, he would have her.

"Ryleigh, huh?"

Martin looked up and grinned at his cousin, Owen. "O, what's up, man?"

Owen took the seat next to him, leaning back and staring out at the crowded dance floor. "I saw you. Over by the bar with Ryleigh earlier. What's that all about?"

"Ryleigh and I are old friends, that's all." He stretched his legs out in front of him. "I was surprised to see her here."

"Her and Ava are like sisters, grew up together."

Martin nodded. "Yeah, that's what she told me."

"Before you kissed her. In the middle of my reception."

Martin shot Owen a look out of the corner of his eye. "You saw that, huh?"

"I did. Where did you two meet?"

Martin explained the project in Brazil and gave him a brief synopsis of their dealings. "You know she lives in Michigan."

Martin knew that. He'd known where she was all along, but

hadn't made contact by choice. "Yeah, I know. But it's not like we were together or anything."

Yet, if he was being honest with himself, he would admit that it had scared him. *She* had scared him. Waking up and finding her gone was one thing. Realizing that he was pissed, and more than a little hurt, was another. For the first time ever, he'd actually gone to sleep looking forward to waking up and eating breakfast with someone. That thought had made him feel vulnerable, and that was some bullshit. Vulnerable and Martin Sullivan didn't belong in the same sentence. And even though he'd thought of her often, he purposefully hadn't called her.

She had no idea he lived less than thirty minutes from her. Sure, she knew he had business in Michigan, that his partner was based in Detroit as well, but he'd only told her that he was from Texas. *We didn't make any promises.* At least, that's what he'd told himself.

Owen eyed him curiously. "Don't you think it's kind of crazy that you met up here? I mean, if you had been in the wedding..."

"I'm sorry about that, O." Martin did feel bad that he hadn't been available when Owen called to ask him to stand up with him as one of his groomsmen. As honored as he'd been to be asked, he couldn't make the commitment at the time. "Work has been hectic. With Carter going through everything, I've had to pick up some of his slack."

Martin's business partner, Carter Marshall, had suffered unimaginable loss after his wife and baby were killed in a fire. The man had retreated into a severe depression, which of course, affected their business.

"I understand. That was devastating."

"Yeah." The loss was palpable, even now. It had been over a year, but Martin still missed his goddaughter and his friend's wife. They'd become a family. When he'd decided to go to college in Michigan, he'd left his entire family behind. He didn't know anyone. Carter was his college roommate. They'd become fast friends. Martin had been Carter's best man at his wedding.

"I'm glad you could make it," Owen said, interrupting his thoughts. "It's been too long."

Frowning, Martin turned to his cousin—his first friend. "Where else would I be?"

Owen shrugged. "I don't know. Traveling around the world, making money. What happened to us getting season tickets for the Cowboys?"

"Man, I haven't been to a game in years."

"That's because you're bullshitting around with them Detroit Lions."

"Ha. Shut the hell up. I can feel it. They're going to make the playoffs this season."

The battle was one he'd never win. He'd never been able to explain his love for the Detroit Lions. Hell, he wasn't even from Michigan, but he'd always been a fan. Not that he didn't root for his home team, "Dem Boyz."

Martin and Owen spent a few moments talking sports and catching up on the goings on in the family. It had been years since the two of them had just sat around and kicked it. They'd come a long way from the awkward boys who'd spent every waking moment together.

Martin let his gaze wander over Ryleigh's curves again before turning his attention back to his cousin. "Are you happy?"

He hadn't meant the question to come out like that, accusing. But he genuinely wanted to know, and hoped the answer would be "yes."

Owen rubbed his chin, then his eyes drifted over to his bride dancing with the other girls on the floor. A wide smile then crept across his face before he nodded. "I am. She's the woman I can't live without."

During their childhood, Martin and Owen had made a pact to never let a "girl" keep them from their goals. They weren't stupid enough, even at the age of ten, to believe they'd be able to stay away from women altogether. But it was always "Cash over ass." Now, Owen was married. Where had the time gone?

Finishing off his drink, Martin leaned back in the chair. "I'm glad. You deserve to be happy."

"I do, don't I?" Owen laughed. "Who knew I'd willingly propose to someone who wasn't Nia Long."

They both burst in laughter. The fight that had ensued when Owen declared that Nia would be his bride one day still made Martin chuckle. As if either of them would ever meet the woman in real life, he'd responded with an unnecessary punch to the gut at the declaration. Next thing he knew, they were rolling around in the grass fighting. After all, Ms. Long was his.

"Ava is beautiful, man." Martin gestured out to the dance floor. "She's perfect for you."

Owen motioned for the waitress to come over.

"She's a virgin."

Martin's eyes flashed to his cousin. "Are you serious?"

The smile on Owen's face, the love shining in his cousin's eyes as he watched his new wife saunter over to them, told him everything he needed to know.

Ava stopped in front of them. "Owen, come dance with me."

Owen kissed Ava's palm. "Can you give me a few minutes to catch up with Martin?"

The beautiful bride smiled at Martin. "I'm glad you could make it. I hope we can see more of you."

"You will," Martin promised. The thrill of work had worn thin. He was ready to slow down, take time to travel for fun, and spend more time with family. His parents were getting older, and he was their only child. They needed him to be around. "Why don't we plan something for the holidays? I'll have some time off."

Owen grinned. "That's perfect. We can definitely make that happen."

"Are you dating?" Ava asked Martin.

Martin's mouth fell open, surprised by the question. So surprised, he couldn't get the words out to answer her. Owen had warned him that Ava was the worst matchmaker in history. Apparently, she'd tried to hook one of her friends up with another cousin of theirs and it was a disaster.

"Babe, no," Owen said. "Don't even think about it. The last time you had that gleam in your eyes, we ended up bailing Larry out of jail."

Ava shrugged. "I was just asking."

"No more hook-ups. Martin is perfectly able to find his own dates."

"Hey, he's cute and successful. I have four beautiful bridesmaids." She pointed to her crew, and Martin immediately locked his gaze on Ryleigh. "I'm thinking..." Ava tapped her chin. "Raven is perfect for you."

"That won't work." Owen elbowed Martin, drawing his attention back to the conversation. "Ava, baby, you owe me a dance. Just give me a few minutes. Please?"

Ava's shoulders fell, disappointment playing on her face. "Okay. A few more minutes. Then, I want to dance with my groom."

Once Ava was out of earshot, Owen groaned. "She's so damn beautiful."

"You're so damn soft. Anyway, what did you say earlier?" He lowered his voice, leaning in closer. "You mean to tell me you and Ava never had sex before?"

Owen shook his head. "No. She wanted to wait until marriage, and I wanted her."

Martin leaned back in his chair, and shook his head. "I don't know how you did it. We're talking years of abstinence here, man. If I had doubts, and I'm not saying I did, I definitely know you're in it for the long haul."

"What can I say? She's worth the wait."

Martin thought about that for a minute. It was something else to see how Owen had changed over the years. "Well, you better go dance with your wife."

Owen stood, held out his hand. Instead of shaking it, Martin stood and pulled him into a hug.

"I'm proud of you, man," Martin said.

Owen stepped back and grinned. "It means a lot to hear you say that. Look, I know we haven't kept in touch like we promised, but I meant what I said. It would be amazing if we got together over the holidays. I want Ava to know you."

Nodding, Martin promised Owen that he would make it happen before watching his cousin walk away and steal Ava from her friends. He eyed the newlyweds as they danced for a minute, before heading toward the bar.

After ordering another drink, he checked his email while he waited for the bartender to bring his cognac.

"Bartender?"

Martin paused and smiled to himself. *I knew it.* He felt her eyes on him, but he didn't acknowledge her. Intent to focus on his phone and not succumb to the lure of her—at least right then—he typed an email response to a client.

The bartender sat his glass in front of him, and Martin gave him a quick glance. "The lady wants a shot of Patron."

"Sure thing," the bartender said.

"How did you know what I was going to order?" she asked.

"I could taste on you." He grinned when he heard her sharp intake of breath, but he still didn't turn to face her.

"You didn't have to do that," Ryleigh told him. "I'm capable of asking for my own tequila."

Martin looked at her then, fighting the urge to tease her. "Just say thank you. It won't kill you."

"Okay, thank you. But you have to take one with me."

He nodded at the bartender. "Go ahead and bring me one."

When the bartender returned with two full shot glasses, she smiled at the young guy before he hurried to another waiting guest. Lifting her glass, she arched a brow. "A toast?"

Martin smirked, raising his glass. "Go for it."

She sprinkled salt on her hand. Then, she turned those brown eyes on him. "To a new adventure." Ryleigh licked the salt off of her hand and took the shot. Picking up the lemon that was hooked onto her small glass, she put it into her mouth and sucked on it.

Damn. He'd been so distracted by her and the way she'd wrapped her lips around that lemon that he forgot he had his own still-full shot glass in the air.

Coughing to clear his throat and his mind, he gently gripped her wrist and brought it up to his mouth. Never breaking eye contact, he bent and licked the rest of the salt off of her hand, enjoying her surprised gasp. He gulped his shot down and slammed it on the counter. *Checkmate.*

RYLEIGH WATCHED Martin suck the same lemon she had before dropping it into the empty shot glass. Shaking her head to clear the haze of desire that had wrapped itself around her, she pondered her next move. Who was she kidding? She craved this man.

She'd done her best to pretend she was unaffected by his presence there. But she hadn't been able to deny it. Twerking, doing old school dances, and laughing with her friends were momentary distractions. Inevitably, she'd found herself looking for him. And every time she had seen him, his eyes had been on hers. It was almost like he was waiting for her to meet his gaze.

Ava had already announced to them that he was single, and then proceeded to tell Raven that she was going to hook them up. Hell to the no. Immediately, she'd tensed up, ready to throw a flag on the play. Fortunate for her, she'd already given Raven the unabridged version of her little fling with Martin, and her friend had rebuffed Ava's attempt at a hook-up. It was then that she'd decided to take matters into her own hands. If anyone was going to "hook-up" with Martin Sullivan, it was going to be her. Period.

Taking a deep breath, she met his waiting gaze, and stepped into him. "Come with me?"

He took a sip of his cognac. "Come with you where?" His gaze dropped down to her lips.

Grabbing the glass from his hand, she set it down on the bar. Stepping up on the tips of her toes, she whispered against his ear, "Do you have to ask?" She grazed her teeth over his earlobe before brushing past him and heading toward the bay of elevators.

The Prescott's had spared no expense. There were no other parties in the massive banquet hall that evening, so it wouldn't be a hard time finding a private place. As Ryleigh neared the elevator, she hoped he'd follow her. *What if he doesn't?*

If he didn't, then she'd underestimated him. If he didn't, then she'd just have to step her game up. Before she could push the button, she felt him come up behind her and push it.

When the elevator door opened, she stepped in and directed the elevator to the fifth floor. As the elevator ascended, she held her breath. He was so close, right behind her. His warm breath on her neck, made her shift on her feet. She was tempted to turn around, let him have his way with her right there, but she didn't move. The bell rang, and the heavy door opened.

Ryleigh led him down the long hall, to the Grand River Ballroom. Pushing the door open, she walked in. Before she could say anything, he had her up against the wall, his mouth on hers, his tongue stroking hers.

His arm snaked around her waist, holding her to him. Thank Goodness, because if it hadn't been there, she probably would have melted into a puddle on the floor. The firm press of his lips against hers, the way he seemed to pour his soul into hers, made her want to weep it was so good. He tasted like the smooth cognac he'd just finished.

Her head fell back against the cool wall and he trailed kisses down her neck to the low cut of her dress, tracing his tongue over her skin. She couldn't breathe. She needed to take control of the situation, but he was working magic over her body, one kiss, one lick, at a time.

"Ryleigh, I'm not going to make love to you in this ballroom," he murmured against her skin.

Her eyes popped open and her brain tried to register his words.

"What?" Was he seriously going to kiss her senseless and then leave her hanging?

He stood to his full height, drew her bottom lip into his mouth, and sucked it. "I know what you want. And I know you're used to getting your way, but not tonight. Not here. When I take you, it's going to be on my terms."

Frustration bubbled in her throat, but she was tongue-tied. She wanted to rail against him, scream at him for winding her up and not giving her the release she needed. But his hands... she felt her dress brushing up her thighs. She groaned at the way he placed wet kisses along her jaw before dipping his tongue into her mouth again.

He pulled her Spanx down, then his fingers were on her hips, flirting over the tender skin of her thighs. Martin knew what he was doing. He'd only pulled her girdle down so much, enough to give him access to her core but not enough to allow her any leeway. He wanted her helpless, needing his touch. And she couldn't stand it. She couldn't stand him. But, shit, she wanted him.

"If I give you what you want, you won't give me what I want." He pushed into her, letting her feel his erection against her belly.

"Martin," she murmured. Or was that a whimper? She couldn't be sure because she damn near wanted to cry.

"What, Ryleigh?"

Oh God, the way he says my name. His voice was like gravel, low and rough.

"Say it?"

"Martin, stop doing this to me. Please?" Yes, she was begging but she didn't care.

"Are you ready to cum?" he whispered against her ear.

"Yes," she breathed.

"Tell me you want me."

"I do."

He whipped her around, pressing her face forward to the wall. The protest died on her lips when he cupped her in his hand.

She cried out his name when he slid a finger over her slit before pushing it into her. Brazenly, she pushed back against him, urging him to move. But his finger stayed still.

"Damn, you're so wet." He ran his tongue down the back of her neck, then bit down lightly. "I want to bury myself inside you and fuck you right here."

Do it.

"It won't take you long." He pushed another finger inside her. "You're right there, Ryleigh."

"Please." Now, that was a whimper.

"Fuck it." He pumped her with his fingers, brushed his thumb against her clit. His hips thrust against her ass as he moved inside her. Her orgasm came quick as waves of pleasure consumed her. Exhausted, she fell back against his chest. When he withdrew his fingers, she let out a low moan, missing the contact immediately.

Martin pulled her Spanx back up and straightened her dress without speaking.

For her part, Ryleigh wasn't sure what she should say. She'd just had a delicious and much-needed orgasm. But it wasn't nearly enough. She wanted more, she wanted him inside her.

"You know you're wrong." She turned to face him, and straightened his tie.

"Breakfast?" he asked. "My phone number has not changed."

Sighing, she nodded. "Breakfast."

The smile he blessed her with shifted something inside of her. "I like feeling you come around my fingers. Next time, you'll come against my tongue."

Ryleigh's mouth fell open, but she recovered quickly, pulling him into an intense kiss. Time to take control of this situation. When she felt him harden against her, she broke the kiss and stepped out of his grasp.

Circling him, she stopped behind him and snaked her arm around his waist. Stroking his growing erection with her hand, she squeezed him through his pants. He hissed out her name and she grinned. "I don't like that you're playing with me. But your tongue against my clit sounds like a game I really want to play. Bring it." With that, she bit his neck gently and strolled out of the room.

3

The next morning, Ryleigh stepped into her favorite spot in town, The Little Rose. It was a cross between Coney Island and a quaint café. Lillian, the owner, had fed Ryleigh more times than she could count, especially when her mother went on a bender. All she'd had to do was walk in the door and Lillian would give her a warm smile and whip up a hearty plate of whatever she desired.

She scanned the dining area, noting that her booth was sitting open. The hostess recognized her immediately and quickly showed her over to her table. She smiled, taking in the room. Not much had changed through the years, save for the new paint job. The chairs were still uncomfortable, but the place felt like home. Lillian poked her head out of the kitchen and smiled at her when she saw her.

"Hey, Ry-girl."

Ryleigh gave her a genuine smile as she walked over to the table. "Mama Lil." She stood up and fell into the older woman's arms. Ryleigh had never met her grandmother, on either side. But if she had to pick one, she'd definitely pick Mama Lil. She was everything Ryleigh had dreamed of when she was young. She still smelled like cinnamon and syrup, with her salt-and-pepper hair styled into a neat bun.

Pulling back, Mama Lil gave her the once over. "You look good, girl," Mama Lil said, her southern twang evident. "Curves in all the right places. I'm glad you didn't go get all crazy with that working out these young people are doing nowadays."

Mama Lil was a thick woman, with full hips and a big ass. She always used to tell Ryleigh that "no man wanted a stick to sleep with." It was Mama Lil that helped Ryleigh embrace her stature. She didn't consider herself fat, but she had never been model-thin like her mother. She was bigger than most growing up and it had given her a complex, especially when her mother stole food from her mouth and berated her food choices every chance she got. Mama Lil had implored her to hold her head high and "swing 'dem hips." The advice had served her well over the years.

"Now, Mama Lil, you have to work out sometimes."

Mama Lil waved a dismissive hand at her. "Girl, I bet you don't have a hard time getting a man to look twice." Mama patted her cheek. "Speaking of, when are you going to bring someone over to meet me? I'm getting old, now. I need to know you're happy."

Ryleigh swallowed. "Don't say that, Mama Lil. You're young as ever."

The years had been good to Mama Lil, but Ryleigh knew the older woman was getting up there in age. The thought of getting that call one day made her shudder with sadness. Aside from Ava and the Prescotts, Mama Lil was one of three reasons she ever returned her hometown. She was her family, and Ryleigh made it a point to check in on her.

"You stop, Ry-girl. Did you get my package?"

Ryleigh nodded. Mama Lil had made Ryleigh the executor of her estate. The older woman had only had one child, who'd died some time ago. A year earlier, she'd called Ryleigh and told her that she was the only one she trusted to not dismantle her legacy in Rosewood Heights. It had touched Ryleigh that Mama Lil trusted her to be there if something happened to her.

"I have everything locked away, Mama Lil." As she let her gaze wander over Mama Lil, she couldn't shake the feeling that the older woman wasn't saying something. "Your lawyer did an amazing job getting everything in order."

"Remind me to tell you about the stash of money I have hidden in the walls. You'll need that if something happens to me."

Ryleigh shot Mama Lil a wobbly smile. "Mama, do you have something to tell me?"

"Nah, honey. I'm just being proactive. I plan on being here for a long time."

Usually direct, it surprised Ryleigh that Mama Lil wouldn't meet her gaze. "Are you sure?"

Mama Lil nodded. "Don't worry about me. Do you want your usual?"

Accepting the change of subject, Ryleigh shook her head. "Coffee for now. I'm meeting someone here."

Smiling, Mama Lil crooned. "Is that someone a man?"

"Mama, please."

"Ooo, girl. You should have said something. Turn around, and let me make sure you have it poppin'!"

No filter. Truthfully, Mama Lil had never had one. It was one of the things Ryleigh loved about her. She told it like it was with no apologies. Laughing, she did a twirl for Mama. When she faced her again, she asked, "Good?"

Mama Lil murmured her approval with a smack on the butt before she trekked back into the kitchen.

Ryleigh took her seat again, glancing at her watch. She'd purposefully arrived early so that she could chat with Mama Lil for a bit before Martin arrived. It was good to see her surrogate Grandma, if even for a little while. Despite how she felt about Rosewood Heights, she'd have to make it a point to come see her more.

Letting her mind drift to Martin, she wondered how he would view their town. She'd planned a day of sight-seeing, visiting all the things that made Rosewood Heights one of the premier resort towns in the area.

A waitress brought over a piping hot decanter of coffee, and poured some for her. Ryleigh wrapped a hand around her mug. She couldn't believe she was there, waiting on Martin. *Breakfast.* If she had any sense, she would have hopped on the first plane out of South Carolina, but she was obviously senseless because she was still there.

Instead of waking up, satisfied from a night full of orgasmic pleasure, she'd opened her eyes in a foul mood. Thinking about her interlude with Martin in the banquet room pissed her off and excited her at the same time. She wasn't an innocent by any means. But no man had left her wanting as much as he had. As frustrated as she was with herself for letting him simultaneously frustrate and turn her out, she'd still texted him first thing that morning with the details for breakfast. After she'd left Brazil, she'd scrolled past his telephone number many times and tried to tell herself she didn't want to call. She'd even tried to delete it, but she never could. He had done something to her that hot night, and Ryleigh couldn't shake it—or him.

This is why I need to take my ass home. Martin Sullivan had already pushed her out of her comfort zone, had her doing things she normally would not do. Breakfast was not for the weak at heart. It wasn't like dinner. Anybody could go to dinner. But breakfast? Eating eggs and bacon with Martin felt like a big step.

Ryleigh was a planner, and breakfast was her favorite meal of the day. She rarely missed it because it was her thinking time. It was the first, most important part of her day, and set the tone for everything. Letting someone share it with her felt like she was opening up a piece of herself and serving it to him on a platter, especially since she'd chosen a place that had personal meaning for her.

I'm too damn busy for this shit. She had responsibilities, damn it. There was just no time to devote to a relationship. Not that he'd asked her to be in a relationship with him. But it seemed like he wanted something from her, and that *something* was more than she could give.

When she was younger, when she was more hopeful, she'd wanted the Happily-Ever-After. It was her only solace, her only reprieve, as Harriet Fields' daughter. There were nights when she'd sit in the dark because the light bill hadn't been paid, and wish for the white knight on a horse to come save her. The man on the horse was her father, initially. But he'd never shown his face in Rosewood Heights again after he left. After years of crying for him, she'd given up on that dream and imagined a handsome man with a bald head and a beautiful smile would come and sweep her off her feet. He'd look like Tupac, only without the Thug Life tattoos.

After a while, even that dream, hadn't helped her escape the booze filled rants of her mother and the slew of leering and questionable men paraded in and out of the house. It wasn't uncommon for her mother to spend hours telling her how useless and ugly she was. Instead of the endearing nicknames most women used when referring to their daughters, her mother took pleasure in calling her "fat ass" in front of anyone who would listen.

Sometimes Ryleigh didn't know how she made it out of her mother's house with her sanity. If it wasn't for her girls and Mama Lil, she doubted she would have amounted to anything. Mama Lil had held her when she couldn't stand, her girls had eaten ice cream with her and hid her when she needed to get away.

When she did finally make it out, she put those girlish, romance novel dreams out of her heart and mind. Ryleigh decided that she didn't need a man to save her because she would save herself. And she wouldn't end up like her mother, falling apart over a man or depending on a man to support her. Not that Ryleigh didn't want to eventually find her equal, either. Sometime in her freshman year of college, after realizing she actually liked sex, she'd vowed to find a companion, someone she wasn't head over heels in love with, but a partner in life. It would be a merger of sorts, to combine talents and keep each other company. And she knew right away that Martin would not fit the bill. Because if she was honest with herself, she could see herself falling for him, and she didn't want to lose herself in love.

That's it. She was officially losing her mind. As far as she knew, he only wanted a few fucks. Despite the flashing danger sign in her mind's eye whenever he was around, she couldn't deny she wanted the same thing. *Wouldn't it be a good way to go out?* Martin behind her, doing her until she couldn't even talk or think. She heard a throat clear behind her and turned. Martin was standing there, a soft smile on his face like he could read her mind.

"Hey, I'm sorry." She motioned to the seat across from her. "I was just..." *Imagining you inside me?* She cleared her throat. "Have a seat."

"Can I get a hug?" He held his arms out.

She stood and walked into his embrace. He was warm, like a cocoon. She found herself relaxing into him, burrowing into his chest, taking from his strength. His hands swept over her back.

"Ryleigh."

She jerked back. *Oh shit.* "Um, I'm sorry. I just lost my train of thought." She rolled her eyes, and cursed herself for letting herself revel in that hug for a second—or four—too long.

He narrowed his eyes as he slid into the booth across from her. "Are you okay?"

Swallowing hard, she nodded. "I'm good. Just thinking about work," she lied. "I have a lot to do."

"When does your flight leave?"

"Tonight. I have to be back in the office tomorrow morning."

He turned over his mug. "Sounds about right."

Martin motioned to the waitress, who bounced right over to the booth, grinning from ear-to-ear. The young woman was obviously impressed with Martin, judging by the way she shifted on her feet and eyed him like he was a celebrity.

Ryleigh couldn't blame the girl, though. It was very rare that someone who looked like Martin walked through those doors. Or any door. She allowed herself a chance to rake over his features as he chatted with the waitress. He was like fine wine, better as the days passed. He wore dark jeans and a T-shirt that showed off his muscular arms and defined chest.

"Ryleigh?"

His voice brought her back to the present. She had to quit daydreaming about this man. "Huh?"

"Are you ready to order?" he asked, with a chuckle.

"Oh." It came out louder than she intended, and she ducked her head to view the menu, not that she needed to. She knew what she wanted. More importantly, Mama Lil knew what she wanted. Giving up the pretense, she told the waitress. "Tell Mama Lil I want my usual."

"Come here often?"

She glanced up at him. "Every single time I come home. Mama Lil, the owner, is a good friend of mine."

"That's cool." He looked around the room. "What is your usual?"

Suddenly nervous, she ducked her head. "I love the blueberry pancakes with thick bacon. Mama Lil always puts extra blueberries in for me. She's actually the only person I'll let make me them."

"How long has this place been here?"

"At least thirty years. I've been coming here all my life. It's home for me."

"In that case, thank you for suggesting it. It must have been hard for you to do that."

There it was again. What scared her the most about Martin was that he seemed to have her pegged from the first time they'd chatted. It was almost like he could *see* her, like she'd opened a window to her soul that only he could access.

The night they'd shared in Brazil had been the best night of her life, with anyone. It wasn't just the sex. They had talked to each other. She'd shared things with him she hadn't told anyone else. Not die hard secrets, but dreams that she'd been too scared to release into the atmosphere. Martin hadn't judged her either. He just listened. She hadn't expected to wake up and feel the blinding fear that accosted her. The only way she could rid herself from the overwhelming anxiety that had set in was to leave. She'd regretted it in the days after, and had been tempted to call him. In the end, she'd left well enough alone.

"Can I ask you a question?" Martin sat back in the booth and sipped his coffee.

"Go ahead."

"Why did you leave?"

MARTIN HADN'T MEANT to bring the past up. The small talk they'd shared a few minutes earlier had done nothing for his curiosity. He had to know, especially after last night. He could have had her, right in the middle of a public ballroom. But he'd made a vow to himself right around the time she approached him at the bar and asked her to come with her. He would not make love to Ryleigh again, not until she was ready to be honest.

Was she as scared as he was? Did she wake up and freak out? Or had he totally misread the situation? Ryleigh was an enigma, almost like a riddle he couldn't quite figure out. And he wanted— no, he *needed* to figure her out.

Martin understood that the night between them had changed him in a way that he wasn't ready for at the time. His mother had once told him that he'd know he found the one when every single woman after her seemed lacking. Trust and believe, Martin had thrown himself into other women after he woke up alone in Brazil. But his mother was right. Sex was good, but it was nothing compared to the night they'd shared. Every woman he'd been with paled in comparison to the one sitting in front of him.

When he saw Ryleigh walking down that aisle during the cere- mony, looking like an angel with glowing skin and the most beau- tiful smile he'd ever seen, it felt like kismet. Almost like some unearthly being had gift-wrapped her and dropped her into his lap. From that moment, she was all he could see. He'd practically stalked her for the rest of the day, waiting for the right time to approach her. That was something he'd never done before. He'd be a fool not to at least try with her.

Ryleigh didn't answer his question right away, so he waited.

The silence stretched on, and time ticked away. He couldn't take it. *Fuck it.* He opened his mouth to speak but an older woman with a wide, almost sneaky, grin approached them.

"Girl, I'm so glad I remembered to pick up more blueberries from the market," the woman said, setting a plate of golden pancakes with fat blueberries in front of Ryleigh. "You know you're the only one I do this for."

Ryleigh grinned, and looked up at the woman. "Thanks, Mama Lil. These smell divine. You spoil me."

The woman shot him a glance, and slid a plate in front of him. The thick pieces of bacon, fried eggs, and hash browns seemed appetizing enough, but he couldn't stop staring at Ryleigh's plate.

"Is this your guy?" the older woman asked.

"No, Mama Lil. This is my friend, Martin. He's Owen's cousin, in town for the wedding. Martin, this is Mama Lil."

Martin smiled and shook the lady's hand. "It's good to meet you. Ryleigh told me you two go way back."

Ryleigh had described the woman as a friend, but considering their age difference and the soft expression in Ryleigh's eyes when she addressed Mama Lil, he wondered if she'd downplayed the relationship.

Mama Lil slid next to Ryleigh, pushing her to the wall. Martin laughed at the heavy sigh Ryleigh let slide out of those lips.

"Is that what she said, huh?"

"Yes, ma'am."

Mama Lil glanced at Ryleigh and elbowed her. "He has manners, Ry-girl." She turned back to him. "I'd like to think I had a lot to do with how my girl turned out. It was touch-and-go for a minute there."

Ry-girl. There was a story behind that name, and he planned to get the scoop. Leaning forward, Martin whispered, "Tell me more."

Ryleigh piped up. "No. No stories, Mama Lil. Don't you have food to cook?"

Mama Lil winked at him, before telling Ryleigh to "hush."

"Come on, Ry-girl," he said with a wink. "I'd love to hear all about some of those touch-and-go moments."

A blush worked its way up Ryleigh's neck to her cheeks. "Can we just enjoy breakfast? I have a full day planned."

Mama Lil squeezed Ryleigh's shoulder. "It's okay, Ry-girl. I won't tell all your secrets. Today." She stood to her feet, and picked up Martin's plate.

"Wait, I—"

"Oh, please," Mama Lil said. "You and I both know you'd rather have Ryleigh's usual." The woman didn't miss a beat. "I'll bring you out a hot plate of blueberry pancakes, extra on the blueberries. Be right back."

Then, she was gone, yelling something at the hostess before disappearing into the kitchen.

Martin looked at Ryleigh, mouth hanging open. "I like her."

Ryleigh's eyes were suspiciously bright and glossy. "I love her."

The admission caught him off guard. From what he knew of Ryleigh, she kept things close to the vest. "Tell me more about her."

She paused before she cut into one of her pancakes. "You really will love these pancakes. I almost feel bad for eating them in front of you. Almost."

He chuckled, her attempt to change the subject not lost on him. "I'll have mine soon enough. So, tell me. How did you become Ry-girl?"

"I have no idea. She just started calling me that one day, and never stopped." She laughed, and his heart opened up just a little. "She's the only one that calls me that, though, so don't get any ideas." She pointed her fork at him for emphasis.

"How did you meet?"

38

Mama Lil picked that moment to emerge from the kitchen with another plate of blueberry pancakes. She gave him a wicked grin, leaned down and placed a kiss to Ryleigh's forehead, and then walked away. "Enjoy," she yelled over her shoulder.

The scent of tart blueberries and batter wafted to his nose and he couldn't wait to try them. Mama Lil had done all the work for him. The butter was already dripping down the pancakes so all he had to do was pour syrup over them, which he did quickly. When he took his first bite, he couldn't help the groan that escaped. He'd never had pancakes that seemed to melt in his mouth.

He chewed, pointing down at his plate. "These are the bomb."

"I told you."

They ate in silence for a few minutes.

"I met her when I was in middle school," Ryleigh said, breaking the silence. "I didn't have lunch money, and I was hungry so I came here."

Ryleigh told him the story of how she'd come into the restaurant one day, begging to wash the dishes for a sandwich and an ice cold soda. Mama Lil hadn't hesitated. "She made me four sandwiches that day and gave me four cans of pop out of her own refrigerator. Then she told me to come back the next day for more."

Martin listened as Ryleigh explained how their relationship grew from there, and admitted that Mama Lil was more like a grandma to her. "So, you never knew your grandparents?" he asked.

Ryleigh shook her head, a pained look crossing her face. "I barely know my parents. My mom…she still lives in town, but I don't hear from her unless she needs money. My father? He left when I was kid and I never saw him again." She shrugged. "Ava's parents were a Godsend, and then there was Mama Lil. I'm thankful that they were there for me."

Martin couldn't relate. He'd had the luxury of having both parents and knowing both sets of grandparents. He couldn't imagine not having that support system. There was no telling where he'd be without them. "Well, as my Granny used to say, 'God put you in the right place at the right time.'"

She eyed him, tilted her head as if she was trying to figure out where he was coming from. "Do you go to church?"

The question was unexpected, but he had no problem answering. "I do sometimes, when I'm home. Growing up, we practically lived at church."

There was Sunday School, Sunday Morning Worship Service, Sunday Afternoon Service, Wednesday Bible Study, Friday Joy Night, Saturday Youth Activities, and choir rehearsal was in there somewhere. Not that he could sing. He was actually tone deaf, the only person in his family that could not string a tune together with ease. That didn't stop his mother from making him sing in the dreaded choir. He cringed when he thought of the hot ass choir robes he'd been forced to wear.

"Really?"

"Don't act so surprised. I'm not a heathen."

She covered her mouth, a smile peeking out from behind her hands. "I'm not...I guess I didn't peg you...I don't know."

"Clean it up," he teased.

"Did your grandmother take you to church?"

"Actually, no." His grandmother rarely went to church. She was the same woman that could quote the bible one minute and cuss someone out the next. But he knew she loved the Lord. "My parents did. My father was a Deacon and my mother was the choir director."

She grinned. "Sounds fun. I used to wish my mom would take me to church."

"I doubt you would have wanted to be in church every day of the week. But I do appreciate my parents for making me go. I can say that the lessons I learned have helped me in adulthood."

"And that's what matters most."

They settled into a comfortable silence this time, as they finished their meal. It was nice. He loved getting to know her, and he wanted to know more.

Once they were ready to leave, she waved the waitress over. "Can you tell Mama Lil that we're going to leave?" Martin went for his wallet, but her hand on his arm halted his movement. He gave her a questioning glance, but she waved him off. "No need to do that."

"You don't have to pay for my breakfast, Ryleigh."

"I won't. You'll see."

Mama Lil breezed over to the table, hands on her hips. "You're not leaving already are you?" She glanced down at Martin. "And don't even think of pulling out your wallet. This one is on me."

Martin relaxed a bit, as he watched a look pass between Mama Lil and Ryleigh. "Thank you, ma'am."

"No need to thank me. My Ry-girl has not paid for a meal in this place since I met her, and she won't start today. And since you're with her, it's your lucky day, too."

Ryleigh stood and leaned down to hug the petite woman. "I love you, Mama Lil. I'll call."

"You better do more than call. Visit. More."

Ryleigh laughed. "I promise."

Martin slid out of the booth, and reached out to shake Mama Lil's hand, but she pulled him into a tight hug.

"You take care of my Ry-girl. I don't know you, but if you're good enough for her to bring you here, you must be special."

Martin shot Ryleigh a glance, before pulling back. "It was good to meet you, Mama Lil."

Mama Lil gave Ryleigh a glance out of the corner of her eye, before steeling those seemingly all-knowing eyes on Martin. "She's a good girl, ya know?"

Martin winked at Ryleigh when she frowned. "I know."

"She won't ask for help, or even for your presence. But you have to be persistent. She's stubborn, got it from me."

Martin chuckled. "Stubborn is an understatement."

Mama Lil whacked him playfully on the arm. He really liked this woman. He suspected she'd have plenty to tell him if he could just get her alone. "Boy, hush." Turning to Ryleigh, she squeezed her hand. "Love you, girl."

The women exchanged another tender hug before Ryleigh led him out of the restaurant.

Martin and Ryleigh spent the day walking through the downtown area, stopping in the many shops. As she strolled through town, he started to understand why it had attracted so many tourists. The people were kind, giving. And they all seemed to know Ryleigh. He'd been treated to free food, sweet tea, and the most decadent desserts he'd ever had.

Ryleigh showed him her high school, and the tree she used to climb to get away. Her favorite pastime was reading. She'd disappear from her life for hours with a book, whether it was in the library, on the beach, or in the grassy field behind Prescott Manor.

The more she talked, the more he understood why she'd bolted from him that night. She hadn't had it easy. From what he could tell, nothing came easy for her. She'd had to work hard to get everything.

She'd glossed over her blood relations, but he assumed it was because there was no love lost there. The relationships she maintained were by her choice, and she'd done that as a protection mechanism. But her eyes lit up when she talked about Ava and the Prescott's, about her girls, and mostly about Mama Lil.

Ryleigh was an intelligent, resourceful woman. She'd graduated in the top five percent of her high school class and undergraduate class. Martin was impressed, by her town, by her tenacity, by her.

Later in the evening, they strolled along the beach walk, as they headed back to his hotel.

"Thank you for showing me your town." He nudged her with his shoulder as they walked. "I feel like you should be a tour guide or something."

She laughed, light and sincere. "This was kind of therapeutic for me. You know, I've spent a lot of years trying to distance myself from this place. But it was good to be here, to see the townsfolk I haven't seen. I forgot how good Mrs. Walker's sweet tea is."

Ryleigh groaned and Martin couldn't help but stare. He knew that once their day was over, her face would be ingrained in his memory. Now, he was cataloguing everything about her, the lines in her forehead that peeked out when she was confused or happy, the mole on her nose, the creases around her mouth when she smiled, the deep dimple in her right cheek.

Reaching out, he brushed his thumb over her dimple. She stilled, peered up at him through long lashes. "What was that for?" she asked, her voice barely a whisper.

"Ryleigh Fields, you're beautiful."

And she was. Her expressive brown eyes were like pools of hot chocolate and her lips were full. Her short haircut accentuated everything he loved about her natural beauty. It signaled a confidence in her that drew him in, almost like she wasn't hiding herself. She knew what she wanted in life, and he could relate because he was the same.

"Martin Sullivan, you're funny."

He barked out a laugh at her unexpected words. "Funny? I'm trying to be serious here."

"Okay." She covered her mouth with a hand. "I feel like I've talked so much today. I'm usually the quiet one."

"Quiet, but observant," he mused. "Something tells me that you speak when you have a reason."

She grinned then, arching a brow. "Very astute, Martin. You're right. And you owe me a secret."

He tilted his head, pinning her with his gaze. "A secret?"

"Yesterday, you said you had a secret."

"Ah, my secret. Wouldn't you like to know?"

"I would. So spill."

Martin wondered what she would say when he told her that she'd wounded him with her antics, that he hadn't been able to get her off his mind. One word. Run. She would bolt so fast his head would spin. So he chose to ignore her question for now.

He stepped closer, let his hand drift down her shoulder. "I want to see you again. I want to take you on a date."

Ryleigh rolled her eyes. "A date? Don't you think we're a little past that? You have seen all my goods."

He chuckled. "You're silly." Pulling her into him, he whispered, "Say yes."

"I'm leaving in a few hours."

"And?"

Ryleigh eyed him warily. "I don't know. I'm not really trying to date anyone right now."

"Why?"

She sighed. "I don't have time. Men want too much time, too much everything. I'm not the woman who sits at home and waits for her man. I don't do expectations well because I always fall short."

Martin frowned. Her statement created more questions than answers. He wondered who made her feel that she wasn't good enough. "Well, then, we have something in common because I'm not expecting anything from you. I just want to know you."

Her mouth fell open and her eyes softened. "What if you don't like what you see?"

There was something about her tone. It was almost a glimpse into her soul. "I already do."

Then, he kissed her. Her lips were soft, yielding. He grazed his tongue over them, and she opened for him willingly, letting him take control. Never before had he wanted a woman like this. He didn't just want her, though. That word seemed small in comparison to the emotions running through his head. He wanted to consume her, needed her to want him just as much. It was torture really, a hard truth that he wasn't really searching for.

She wrapped her arms around him, pulled him even closer to her. Her soft mewls seeped into his skin, into his heart, as the kiss intensified. It would be so easy for him to take her back to his room and have his way with her. Ryleigh was willing, ready for him to do just that. He wouldn't, though. Not until *he* was ready.

Yes, he wanted to feel her body under his, feel the warmth from inside her. But more than that, he needed to be sure that when he woke up the next morning, she would be there.

Reluctantly, he broke the kiss, taking in a calming breath. Leaning his forehead against hers, he closed his eyes. *She's going to be the death of me.* That realization struck him, and he backed away completely, needing the distance.

She stood, her fingers on her lips, her eyes dazed. He wanted to go in for more, tease her until she begged for mercy.

"I want you." Her eyes flashed to his. "You already know that." If his words hadn't convinced her, he supposed the bulge in his pants did.

"Martin, I—"

"One date, for one secret." He was playing dirty, and he couldn't care less.

"I have to go. It's a long ride to the airport, and I don't want to miss my flight."

Martin couldn't find any words to convince her to stay. He still hadn't told her that he lived in the Detroit area. But there was a small part of him that wanted to wait, see what she would do. Would she follow through?

"I enjoyed today," she added. "One date. Call me."

Ryleigh walked away before he could respond. He watched the sway of her hips and wanted to bang his head against a wall for letting her slip through his fingers. He could have been buried deep inside her, and not watching her disappear. "Safe travels, Ryleigh," he shouted.

She waved without turning to look at him. "Bye, Martin."

Damn. But at least he'd managed to get her to agree. One date. Martin knew what this meant, and for once, he wasn't afraid to admit it. This date would change everything.

4

If Martin's granny was alive, he imagined she'd tell him he was busier than a cat covering up shit. And he would have to agree with her. He'd spent the better part of the morning plotting, trying to finagle a "surprise" meeting with Ryleigh at her office. He'd moved several meetings around and contacted one of her co-workers to find out where she'd be that afternoon.

He tried to tell himself that he wasn't being disingenuous because he really had no good reason to run into Ryleigh today. After the product launch they'd worked on together, he'd moved on to another project and left one of his employees with her company. From all accounts, Phil was doing an excellent job and there was no need for him to step in.

"Are you sure this is going to work?" he asked Aisha, his Chief Operating Officer and friend. "Why can't I just call her?"

"You already tried that," she said, patting him on his back. "And she told you she was sick, and then proceeded to not call you back."

This was new to Martin. He wasn't the "game playing" type. He tried to always shoot straight from the hip. Except, Ryleigh wasn't playing fair. "You're enjoying this, aren't you?"

Aisha laughed. They'd been friends for years. She was, after all, Carter's sister. The fact that she was even helping him wasn't lost on him. Aisha had made it a point to stay out of his love life. Carter told him once that it was because *she* wanted to be his love interest. Martin didn't believe it, though. Aisha was smart enough to realize that they would rip each other apart if they were a couple. And not in a good way. Great friends, but not compatible at all.

"Hey, I'm just trying to help you out. You can't call her because that would make you seem pathetic."

"Thanks."

"Seriously, I would think you're a punk if I were her."

Narrowing his eyes, he grumbled, "Shut up. Maybe she really was sick, and is now catching up."

"Keep telling yourself that."

Martin didn't know what to think. He thought they'd had a good day together. He'd learned about her hometown, and she seemed to let her guard down with him. Besides, he wasn't *that* guy. He didn't get all crazy over any woman.

But he'd dreamed about her, envisioned her face during meetings. Still, he didn't want to come off too eager, too pressed. Ryleigh wasn't like any woman he'd pursued, not that he'd pursued any woman. He usually didn't even have to do any of the heavy lifting. Women came after him, sometimes with a vengeance.

Maybe that's what made him want to pursue Ryleigh? She wasn't so enamored with his money and his title that she'd drop her pants just because he smiled at her and bought her dinner. In fact, he knew if any pants were dropped it would be because she wanted it. Sure, he could sway her stubborn mind with a few well-placed kisses and strategic touches, but Ryleigh would make the ultimate choice. The ball was firmly in her court. But damn if he didn't want to steal that ball.

"Look, I get it," Aisha said, as though she read his mind. "You're not used to working hard for a woman's affection. But from everything you've told me, this woman is special. So, woo her. Go after her. If you don't, you'll regret it."

Martin knew his friend was right. Ryleigh was special. She'd left an imprint on his brain, a lasting impression that he couldn't shake. "Fine. I'll go, but this feels like too much."

"What feels like too much?" Carter walked into the office. Martin watched his best friend take a seat, as if he'd been holding the world on his shoulders. He slumped into the chair and closed his eyes. "What have I missed?"

"Are you good?" Martin said, ignoring Carter's question.

Carter opened his eyes, stared up at the ceiling. "Today was hard." His friend cleared his throat and then met his gaze. "His lawyer has filed yet another motion to dismiss."

Aisha groaned. "Not again."

Martin nodded, his heart hurting for his friend, his brother. He couldn't imagine the pain Carter was going through. It hadn't been that long since Carter had lost his wife, Krys, and their infant daughter, Chloe, in a fire. Martin wasn't sure his friend would come out of the haze of grief, and now he'd been forced to deal with a long trial. The arsonist that had set the flame was the son of one of the most powerful business owners in the City of Detroit. Of course, because of that, the case hadn't been as open-and-shut as they'd hoped.

"Do you need me to come with you to court?" Martin asked.

Carter shook his head. "What I need is a little peace and a good night's sleep. That's probably too much to ask."

"You could always take the sleeping pill that your doctor ordered," Aisha suggested.

Martin knew Carter wouldn't do it, though. He wouldn't if he was in the other man's shoes. It was a man thing. Aisha would never understand the need to be in control.

"So, what were you two talking about?" Carter asked, changing the subject again.

"Martin is infatuated with this woman who isn't giving him the time of day," Aisha offered, with a wink.

"Aisha is full of shit." Martin glared at her. "Ryleigh will give me the time of day, if I can catch up to her," he grumbled under his breath.

Carter smiled. "Oh, so there is a woman. Finally."

"I have to go." Martin stood, unwilling to get into another conversation about Ryleigh. "I'm headed to a meeting."

"Is this meeting about anything I need to know?" Carter asked.

Martin's shoulders fell. Under normal circumstances, Carter would be handling the majority of company meetings as Martin preferred to be in the trenches, working at the work sites. "Not really."

Aisha met Martin's concerned gaze, her eyes glistening with unshed tears. It had been months since Carter was able to conduct normal business. Martin and Aisha had managed to keep everything afloat, and he'd do it again in a heartbeat for his friend.

"He's right," Aisha said. "We have everything under control. You just let us know if you need us to come with you to trial."

"I'm fine." Carter clenched his hands into fists. "I just need to get back to work."

"Bruh, I know you're fine, but I also need you to handle this." Martin squeezed Carter's shoulder. "You need to see this through until the end."

And Martin hoped that once the trial was over, Carter would be able to get back into the swing of things. He hoped his best friend would be able to live again. The man in front of him was a shell of the man who'd helped him build their consulting company from the ground up. Martin needed Carter to be at the top of his game so they could accomplish their shared goals as a company.

Martin packed up his messenger bag and walked to the door. Turning around, he said, "Aisha, if this backfires, I'm coming for you." He heard her laughter as he strolled to the elevators.

The mood in Campus Martius Park in downtown Detroit was indicative of the positive changes taking place in the "D", as they called the city. The urban park had become a popular spot in recent years, where people gathered to eat, chill, and listen to various performers. Located right in the heart of downtown, Martin walked through the busy park on his way to Ryleigh's office building. The smell of tacos and the sounds of people happily enjoying the fall weather brought a smile to his face.

In the summer, live performances and beach parties brought people from the outlying suburbs into downtown. During the winter months, the ice rink would open and families would descend to the area to enjoy the many activities the city offered, like the annual tree lighting ceremony. Even though, Martin wasn't from Detroit, the city and its people had embraced him like he was. And it would always hold a special place in his heart.

Martin entered Ryleigh's office building and headed straight for the elevators. Just as he rounded the corner, he saw Ryleigh step off the elevator. When she spotted him, she tripped and dropped her drink on the floor.

Smiling, he rushed over to her and knelt down to help her pick up her mess.

"Shit, shit, shit," she mumbled, taking her napkins and soaking up her iced coffee.

"Let me take that," he said, motioning toward her cup.

"What are you doing here?" she spat, through clenched teeth.

"Meeting," he lied before he could stop himself. Closing his eyes, he cursed Aisha out in his head.

She stood and tossed her empty cup into a nearby waste bin. Without looking at him, she pulled a bottle of hand sanitizer from her purse and poured some into her palm. When she was done, she offered her bottle to him and he did the same.

"Where's your meeting?" she asked, still avoiding eye contact.

"Feeling better?" he asked.

A blush crept up her neck and she smoothed a hand over the back of her hair. "Yes. It must have been a twenty-hour bug."

"Ah." He could tell she was lying, so he told himself that his lie wasn't so bad.

Crossing her arms over her breasts, she met his waiting gaze. "I wasn't sick," she admitted. "I mean, I was. But not as bad as I had made it seem."

Sighing, Martin confessed, "I didn't have a meeting. I came here to see you."

The corner of her mouth quirked up, and a grin followed. "Really?"

"You didn't call me back. And I wanted to see you, without seeming like a stalker."

Ryleigh laughed then, and he found himself laughing with her. "I would never peg you for a stalker."

He reached out and ran his thumb over her chin, enjoyed the way her eyes fluttered closed at the contact. "Where were you headed?"

"I was headed out for a walk to get something to eat for lunch."

"Can I join you?"

With her full dimples on display, she nodded. "Sure."

RYLEIGH SAT down on one of the seats in the RiverWalk Garden Rooms area. The Detroit River Walk is a five-and-a-half-mile prom-enade that extends along the Detroit River. It was one of Ryleigh's favorite places in the city, a place where she could relax. She'd often walk the path during her lunch breaks, or sit and watch the water.

"It's nice out here," Martin said, once he took the seat next to her.

They'd stopped at the Panera and grabbed sandwiches and chips for lunch. Ryleigh recalled how he'd argued her down about where they would eat. He wanted to take her to Andiamo's for lunch, but she wasn't the type of woman that had to be wined and dined. Andiamo's was nice, but it was too heavy for such an early meal. If she'd had her way, they'd stop at one of the hot dog vendors along the way to eat. So, they'd settled on Panera.

"I love it. It's so peaceful." She took a bite of her sandwich and watched him out of the corner of her eye. He really was a beautiful man, with his smooth skin and strong features. Exhaling, she thought about his magical hands and the way he'd touched her, almost as if she was a priceless treasure.

Ryleigh didn't have a good reason for not calling him like she'd said she would. Yes, she could argue that she was busy at work because she'd been swamped since her return from Rosewood Heights over a week ago. But she knew the real reason was because she was afraid. Their time together, the day they spent touring Rosewood Heights, was an amazing day. She hadn't had such a perfect day before. Ever. Sure, she'd had good days, but sharing her hometown with him had done something for her that she never imagined.

Growing up, she hadn't appreciated the charm of her town because she'd always viewed it like a prison due to her circumstances. She'd spent so much time running from it, avoiding the pain that pierced her heart when she saw the "Welcome to" sign, that she completely glossed over the good. Ryleigh had met some of the most important people in her life because she lived in Rosewood Heights. They were people who made her life worth living. And she was grateful for that.

Seeing the town through Martin's eyes had been an eye-opening experience. Being with him was like someone had cleaned a dirty window and allowed her to see the beauty she'd been hell bent on ignoring. Mrs. Oak made the best blueberry muffins she'd ever tasted, and there was nothing like the smell of the ocean that permeated the air there. From the vast expanse of green fields to the beach, Rosewood Heights was a beautiful, cultured, haven. Realizing that, and knowing all she had gone through at the hands of her mother, was overwhelming.

"What's on your mind?" Martin asked.

She offered him a tentative smile. "Just thinking about home."

"Really? You're homesick?"

Chuckling, she said, "Two weeks ago, I would have said hell no."

"And now?" He took a sip of his iced green tea. "This tea is good as hell."

She laughed, remembering how she had to practically pull his leg to try it when they were placing their orders. "I told you. Don't sleep on the green tea."

"Damn. I should have got a larger size." He laughed. "Sorry. So, what would you say now about being homesick?"

Ryleigh shrugged. "I wouldn't move back, but now I'm feeling a little nostalgic for home."

"Hm. I wonder why?"

She glanced at him. *You.* "I don't know. And I'm a little worried about Mama Lil."

"Is she okay?"

After she'd returned home, Ryleigh had talked to Mama Lil every day about one thing or another. And each time she'd heard the older woman's tired voice, her stomach did odd flips. She was worried, but she was trying not to be. "I don't know. She says she is."

"And I bet that's the end of the conversation."

"Pretty much. How did you know?"

Shrugging, he told her, "It's the same way with my granny. She says she's fine and I 'better not ask her anymore.'"

Ryleigh thought his grandmother sounded a lot like Mama Lil. "Maybe I'm just tired."

"You do work a lot."

Bumping her shoulder into his, she said, "Hey, I don't work anymore than you do."

"Touché."

"I guess that's one thing we have in common."

When his heated gaze met hers, she felt it all the way down to her toes. *Will this man always affect her like this?* She held her breath as he ran his finger down her cheek. Time seemed to stop, and she wondered if she should say something.

As if he read her mind, he pulled his hand away and she took another bite of her sandwich. "I've come to realize that work will always be there." He smirked before taking a sip of his tea. "Work doesn't warm you up at night."

Ryleigh choked.

He patted her back as she struggled to get the food down. "Are you okay?"

Finally, she nodded and took a huge gulp of tea. "I'm fine."

"Good. Wouldn't want to have to use the Heimlich on you. Not that I don't want to put my arms around you."

Her mouth fell open. "Martin, you're just putting it all out there, huh?"

"I have nothing to lose. I already admitted that I came to your job looking for you."

And that simple fact endeared him to her even more. "I'm sorry I didn't call."

"I am, too."

"I don't know what it is about you that makes me want to run," she admitted. "We barely even know each other."

"You know, that can be remedied if you'd let me take you on an actual date."

"Okay, okay. I promise that I won't flake out again."

Martin scooted close to her, the heat of him enveloping her like a warm blanket. He wrapped his arm around her shoulder and leaned in, whispering in her ear. "I hope not. I promise I'll be on my best behavior?"

She arched a brow. "Really? I was hoping you'd show me your naughty side."

He barked out a laugh. "Oh, trust me, you'll see that soon enough."

Her eyes dropped to his mouth, and leaned forward. She felt his breath on her lips and they parted in anticipation. Only he didn't kiss her. Instead, he finished off his green tea, and winked at her with a gleam in his eyes.

She swatted him on his shoulder playfully. "You are so foul for that."

"What?" he asked innocently.

"Oh, finish your sandwich. I have to go back to work."

As they finished their lunch, they talked about the Detroit Lions and The Dallas Cowboys, Thanksgiving and Black Friday. And she realized that spending time with him didn't only make her realize her love for Rosewood Heights. Being with him, even for that short while, made her long for more time, more stories, more...him.

5

─────────

I*s this payback?*

Ryleigh wanted to scream. It had been a week since she'd had lunch with Martin and she was going crazy. Crazy with need for that damn man. *He came looking for me, damn-it!* He'd left her wanting more, asked her out on another date, and then proceeded to *not* call her. If he was standing in front of her, she'd kick his ass.

She knew he was trouble. *With a very impressive dick attached, if I remember correctly.*

"Ryleigh, you're late for your meeting."

Grumbling a curse, Ryleigh glanced up at the department's administrative assistant, Torie. "What time is the meeting again?"

"Eleven o'clock." The perky woman glanced at the Smart Watch on her wrist. "With downtown traffic, you need to leave now."

"Can I skip this?"

Torie knew Ryleigh's schedule better than she did. She was blessed to call her a friend because Torie had saved her ass more times than she could count.

"No, you can't. It's a huge deal."

Groaning, Ryleigh stuffed a notebook into her purse and shut down her computer. "I need a vacation."

"You just took one."

"A real vacation. Going home for a weekend and two days is not a vacation." Especially when she'd worked her ass off for the wedding planner from hell.

Of course, it was Ryleigh's own fault because she'd refused to take the whole week, like everyone else did. She could have stayed back in Rosewood Heights for a few more days, spent time with Mama Lil and… *Don't even think his name, Ryleigh.*

Torie sat down in front of the desk. "Girl, are you okay? You've been more irritated than usual since you got back from the wedding."

Ryleigh considered that statement a moment. Since she'd returned, she'd thrown herself into work. It had been a futile attempt to get Martin out of her head. She'd practically thrown herself at him at the reception, and he didn't bite. Instead, he'd treated her to a delicious orgasm with his fingers. Then, he'd met her for breakfast, spent a glorious day with her and gave her arguably the best kiss she'd ever received. He'd tracked *her* down and had lunch with her, got her to agree to a date again, and didn't even give her a goodbye kiss. Then nothing. No sex, no call. *Ugh.*

"Ry, you've been so distracted. Everything okay at home?"

Ryleigh thought about Mama Lil. "I guess. I just…" Could she tell Torie about the Will and her estate? *Can I tell her about Martin?* "One of my favorite people in the world made a decision that worries me. I'm just wondering how I can get her to open up to me."

Which wasn't totally a lie. She was worried about Mama Lil and the fact that she kept reiterating instructions for when she is "no longer here." It just wasn't the only thing that had her distracted.

Torie placed a hand on top of hers. "Oh, I'm so sorry. You're not used to worrying, so I understand why you're so frazzled."

Frazzled. "I wouldn't call it that. But I can admit I've had a lot on my mind and on my plate."

"Well, then a vacation is definitely something to consider after this project is done. You need time to decompress."

"Sure." Ryleigh stood. As cool as Torie was, she wasn't sure she could open up to her about her problems. She needed a call. An emergency one with her girls. They usually scheduled one every month. With the wedding and all the celebrations, they hadn't had to do it over the past few months. A bridal shower in Rosewood Heights and a bachelorette party in Cozumel were their last two get-togethers. Phone call not needed. But now…she needed one, and fast.

"Your meeting will last until one o'clock. Don't forget to get lunch because you do have a three o'clock meeting."

Ryleigh rolled her eyes. She hated meetings, especially Friday meetings. They were a huge waste of time, in her opinion and most could be avoided with a simple email. She was convinced meetings were just a way to feel important and talk about the same shit ad nauseam. "I have a better idea. Cancel my afternoon. After this meeting, I'm going home. I don't feel well."

Torie's eyes widened. Probably from the shock of Ryleigh actually taking an unplanned afternoon off. She could count on one hand the times she'd called in sick and that was because she had freakin' pneumonia and was admitted to the hospital. Other than that, she was at work.

Her life had become pretty routine. Work, home, bed. In that order. If someone would have asked her if she was happy a few days ago, she would have responded with a resounding "yes." Now, she wasn't so sure. Time in the office didn't give her the same thrill it once had. There was something missing, and she prayed to God that something had nothing to do with the unmentionable man that showed up in her life wedding and knocked her off her square.

"O-okay," Torie stuttered. "I'll do that. Please let me know if you need anything."

"I will." Ryleigh packed her laptop and her project file into her bag. "I'll see you Monday morning. I'll have my cellphone on, if you need to reach me this afternoon."

Torie followed her out to the elevators. "Hopefully, I won't need to use it. Things have been pretty quiet."

Suddenly unsure of her decision to skip the afternoon at work, Ryleigh ran through all the things she had pending in her mind. And basically, everything she could think of could wait until next week. The world would not end if she wasn't glued to her desk.

"I'll see you Monday." She waved at her assistant and leaned back against the wall of the elevator. Yes, a call was definitely on the agenda.

Stretched out on her sofa later on, Ryleigh yawned. An afternoon free of office politics, fake smiles, and spreadsheets was exactly what the doctor ordered. She'd done nothing but watch television since she'd walked in the door earlier. As far as she was concerned, there was nothing better than Netflix and Ice Cream.

Halfway through her binge watch of House of Cards, she felt her phone buzz from beneath her leg.

"Hello?" she answered without glancing at the screen.

"Hey, doll."

She sat up straight, as if he could actually see her. "Martin. Hey!" The chipper hello wasn't convincing even to herself. Cursing inwardly, she struggled to think of something less desperate sounding. "What's up?"

What's up? Seriously lame.

"Are you busy?" he asked, his voice low and husky in her ear.

Irritation, mixed with a heavy dose of attraction flared through her. Was she busy? The old Ryleigh would have said "Hell, yeah, I'm busy. Get in where you fit in." But this new Ryleigh, the one that had checked her voicemail multiple times a day, the one that had dreamed of his lips and his hands said, "No."

What the hell is wrong with me?

"Get dressed. I'm taking you out."

Ryleigh stood, running to her room. "What makes you think I want to go out with you tonight?"

Who was she kidding? She wanted to go out with him, she wanted it more than she wanted her television shows and her Pralines and Cream ice cream.

"Do you?"

And you can't just call me on a whim and expect me to drop everything to go out with you. Yeah, she didn't say that. She could barely talk as she searched through her closet for the perfect dress and shoes. "If I were to agree to go out with you, where would you take me?"

"If I told you, it would spoil the fun."

She bit down on her thumb nail. "And what should I wear?"

"Is that a yes?"

She paused. It wouldn't hurt to let him wait a few more seconds. "I guess I can move some things around."

"Good. Wear something comfortable."

Comfortable? "Does that mean heels or flats?"

He laughed then, a slow and loaded chuckle. "As much as I want to see those gorgeous legs of yours in stilettos, I think it would be best to wear a good pair of Nikes and jeans."

Hm? Sneakers and jeans. Ryleigh couldn't help but appreciate him even more. A date that didn't consist of uncomfortable clothes and high heeled shoes was right up her alley. "Okay. When should I be ready?"

"One hour. I just need your address."

"I'll text it to you."

She hung up and went to work. *Maybe my night will end better than my morning after all.*

Martin arrived at Ryleigh's condo on time. He sat out in the car for a few minutes, thinking about possibilities. He'd had every intention on calling her before that day. But he'd had to hop on a flight to Minnesota to put out fire for work. Everything that could have happened, did happen. Carter had been understandably missing in action, preoccupied with the court case involving the arsonist that set the fire that killed his family. And with Aisha on vacation, Martin had to take care of everything, which wasn't so bad. He loved his job, especially loved the money he made, but he wondered if he could do this for the rest of his life.

Computers had been a salvation for him. When he was young, he'd become enamored with the inner workings of computers and taught himself to code. Eventually, his parents caught on and had signed him up for several camps and classes. He'd made a living writing code, developing software.

The world wide web held many temptations for him. He rarely talked about it, and only a few people knew that he'd also dabbled in hacking. He was so good that he'd been courted by the Federal Government to work for them. Turning that opportunity down to start a business with Carter was something he wanted to do. And he didn't regret it. He just wanted more. Yet, he wasn't sure if the *more* he wanted had anything to do with his job.

Over the last few months, he'd become very aware that the life he was leading wasn't cutting it. He found himself brainstorming ideas to keep his head in the game of the business but ultimately he knew that there was something missing. *Is it Ryleigh?*

The question had dogged him since he saw her at the wedding. While he was gone, he'd wanted to call her, but he'd been in a foul mood and felt it best that he waited until he got back to town to reach out. He'd approached their date as if he would an important project. Planning. He figured she'd expect him to take her on a fancy date, but he didn't want to do what she expected so when his boy gave him tickets to a Detroit Pistons game, he knew it would be perfect since Ryleigh loved sports.

Ryleigh lived in Dearborn, Michigan, which was about nine miles from the city of Detroit and the eighth largest city in Michigan. It was also only twenty-five miles from his home. He wondered what she would say once he told her that he did, in fact, live in Michigan.

She'd texted him earlier and told him to text when he got there and she would come out. But he got out of the car and walked to her door.

"Hey," she said when she opened her front door. "I would have come out."

"That's not what a good date allows a woman to do."

She held the door open for him, and he stepped into her place. It was cool, like she'd been running the air conditioner all day. "I'll be ready in a few." She motioned toward a sofa in the living room. "Have a seat?"

He took a look around, noting the artwork on the walls and the sculptures placed on various settings. He picked up one of the pieces, a marble piece. Martin was a collector of all forms of art, and wondered if Ryleigh would enjoy attending an exhibit at the Charles H. Wright African American Museum with him next month.

"It's a replica of a piece that was featured in an exhibit called Shadow Matter." He glanced over at her. She was standing under the archway leading to the back of her condo. She shifted from one foot to another, toying with the hem of her shirt. She was dressed in a pair of skinny jeans that fit her like a second skin and an oversized shirt. Her feet were bare. "The artist is M. Scott Johnson. He's amazing. I met him through a friend a few years ago in New York."

"It's a brilliant piece. What's it called?"

"The Tao of Physics. I fell in love with it, and he was kind enough to do a smaller version for me? Of course, it's not exactly the same, but I love it."

Martin set the work back on the glass table. "I'm going to have to check him out."

"You totally should."

He ran a finger over a painting on the wall. It was an oil painting, one so vivid that he couldn't take his eyes off of it. The rich purple, red, and pink were visually stunning and accentuated the design of the room. Judging by her walls and her throw pillows, he assumed she loved the color purple. "This is brilliant. You love purple."

She grinned. "I do." Next to him now, she peered up at the painting. "This one was created by my college roommate. She's going to be big time; I can feel it. I keep telling her it's time to step out there and make some money doing what she loves."

"She definitely has talent."

He turned to her, struck by the need to kiss her in that moment. Martin knew she would let him, too. It was in her eyes—always the eyes.

"Ready?" she asked. "Are you going to tell me where we're going?"

"Are you going to let me handle this, and just enjoy the ride?"

"Ha Ha." She picked up her purse and slung it over her shoulder. "Fine. I'll just be quiet and let you do your thing. I look okay, right? Not overdressed?"

He bent lower, and gave her a kiss on the cheek over her dimple, lingering there for a beat longer than he should have. Long enough to make his body burn with need to get even closer.

"You're perfect."

Ryleigh ducked her head as a blush overtook her flawless skin. "Thank you."

Hours later, they were back at her condo, and Martin didn't want the night to end. The Detroit Pistons won the game and Ryleigh would go down in history as the best date he'd ever had. She'd surprised him countless times throughout the evening, starting with the huge smile on her face once she realized what they were doing. A woman after his own heart, she knew every play, every player, and every penalty. She cheered louder than him. Yep, she was a Pistons fan.

"Want to come in for a drink?" She asked.

Not that he needed one. He was high on her. Martin nodded. "I was hoping you'd ask."

Once they were settled on her sofa, he leaned back, admiring how cozy her place was. He felt comfortable, like he belonged there.

Ryleigh traced the rim of her glass. "I have to say, Mr. Sullivan, you surprised me. I didn't think you'd call."

"Well, then you don't know me. I did track you down at your job last week. I would have called sooner but I had a work issue I had to handle."

"Is that why you're in town?"

Martin hesitated, and chose his words carefully. "I'm curious. Where do you think I live?"

She shrugged. "I don't know. I know you have business in the Detroit area, and that you're here a lot, but I assumed you lived in Atlanta or something. You strike me as a southerner."

He laughed. "I'm from the south, but no I don't live down south."

"Okay, now I'm curious. Where do you live?"

"Canton."

She jerked her head back, her eyes wide. "Canton? As in Canton, Michigan?"

"Yes."

"Wow. I feel so stupid. I can't believe you've been a quick thirty-minute drive away this entire time."

This woman was a breath of fresh air. He wasn't sure how she would react to his "secret" but he didn't expect her to be so fine with his deception. "Would that have changed how you left things in Brazil?"

Being in the rare position of not being in control had been uncomfortable for him then. They'd never agreed to be anything other than the night they'd shared. Over the last several hours, though, he'd quickly come to realize that the night they'd spent together was nothing compared to the time he'd spent with her since then, in Rosewood Heights, having lunch on the River Walk, and today. He didn't even know her then—not like he did now.

She cleared her throat, scratched the back of her neck. "Honestly?"

"Of course." He took a sip of his cognac. "Is there any other way?"

Tucking her legs under her, she sighed. "Probably not."

He laughed then. Her honesty was refreshing. It was refreshing. "Care to elaborate?"

Again, she shrugged. "I can't explain it. I'm just me, and at that time, I wouldn't have stayed even if I knew you lived around the corner."

"That's honest."

"Life hasn't been easy for me, Martin. I've had to work like hell to get everything I have. My mother was never very motherly and my father was basically the local drug dealer who knocked her up after she bargained with her body for a joint and a beer."

Her story would be a contradiction in some's eyes. She'd taken the little her parents did give her and carved out her own success, her own vision. He wanted to encourage her, say something that would let her know that he saw her and he understood the sacrifices she'd made. But the words seemed hollow.

Truth be told, he hadn't had to struggle or beg or rob "Peter to pay Paul" like his Granny used to say. His parents were well-respected, well-educated, and well-paid. As a result, the chances he had in life were set up for his success. Ryleigh hadn't been that lucky.

"Listen, I'm not telling you this as some sort of attempt to gain your sympathy." Ryleigh drummed her fingers over the cushion of sofa. "It isn't an excuse either. But I learned a long time ago not to assume that someone cares about you just because they take you to bed. Words are empty without the actions to back them up."

"True." *That's it*? Ryleigh had just shared something profound about herself with him and he couldn't muster up a better response?

"I know it's not a good answer to your question," she continued. "But it's all I have."

In other words, he'd better accept it or move on. Martin shifted and turned to her, placing a hand on hers. "What about today? Would you stay?"

Finishing her drink, she blessed him with one of her smiles. "Well, you're at my place. I have to stay."

Is that an invitation?

"And to answer your question." Ryleigh flipped her hand, linking their fingers. "About today? I don't know. I can't say for sure."

The room descended into silence. Martin wanted to say more, to ask more questions. He wanted to know everything about her. But he figured it was best to leave it alone because if he told her what he was really thinking, she'd probably freak out.

"I better go," he said finally.

Her hand on his arm halted his retreat. "Please, don't. Stay."

6

—————

Pork bacon was ten times better than turkey bacon, *A Different World* inspired her to go to college, the current President was an incompetent asshole, and driving while black was not for the weak at heart. Those were some of the things Ryleigh knew for sure. Now, she could add *Martin Sullivan is one sexy muthafucka.*

How else could she explain why she'd stopped him from leaving? Shit, she'd enjoyed her date. *Free food is always a plus.* Hell, she loved basketball. *A Friday-night game at the new Little Caesars Arena is a bonus.* Damn, her clothes were still on and her legs were closed. *Even better.* Except, it wasn't better. Not when all she wanted him to do was pull her onto his lap. *Or better yet, his waiting dick.*

Now, as he stared down at her hand on his arm, a feeling she couldn't quite name expanded in her. It was unlike anything she'd ever felt before. Well, actually, she knew the name. There were several. Admiration. Longing. Fascination. Need. Martin had the uncanny ability to throw all her rules in the air and let them fly around like a deck of cards in the wind. Being near him, sitting next to him, made her want to burrow under him. It also made her want to do things to him. Sweaty, freaky things. All night.

It wasn't just about sex, though. She wanted Martin, yes. But she didn't just want him to screw her. That would be the *true* bonus. No, it was about the connection they'd shared. It had been building in Brazil, the tentative friendship they'd started. Instinctively, she knew he was different. Spending time with him had cemented that fact.

Men and relationships were hard work. Either she was downplaying her success to make them feel better or pretending that she was a delicate little flower that would wilt if the dude spanked her. Truth was, she made good money and she loved a man that could make her body sing with the filthy words that came out of his mouth.

The men that she'd "dated" only wined and dined her to get something. The dates would most likely end with a quick uneventful fuck and a cheesy line promising to "keep in touch." It was a huge waste of time. With Martin, though, he seemed to like that she was her own woman, and didn't hold her ambition against her.

Martin was quiet, but strong. He wasn't the type of man that had to tell everyone he was a boss. He just was. It made her yearn for him even more.

"Please," she croaked, unable to stop the need from bleeding into her tone. "I want you to stay."

Ryleigh stood on shaky legs, with no idea what he'd say. Would he tell her "thanks but no thanks?" She wasn't sure she could stand the rejection, not that she didn't deserve it for behaving the way she had in Brazil, and even after she'd left Rosewood Heights and failed to call him like she'd promised.

The heat of his stare, the fire in his eyes, seared her skin. She wasn't blind. Martin wanted her, but this was a man that was very much in control of his words and his actions. Even if he wanted her, they wouldn't take the next step until *he* was ready.

The attraction that she felt for him had the potential to drown her. Even now, she could feel him pulling her under with just his presence. But she wasn't scared, not like she had been in Brazil or even a few weeks ago.

Please, don't go.

He jerked her to him, pulling her flush against his hard body. A moan broke through, almost tearing through her throat when he traced her lips with his tongue before kissing her fully, possessively. She had no choice but to give in, to let him have his way with her.

Wrapping her arms around him, she pulled herself up on the tips of her toes to give him better access. The feel of his tongue on hers, stroking, teasing, was intoxicating. *Damn, this man could kiss my panties off.* And that was exactly what she hoped he'd do.

She caressed his face, as Martin nipped at her mouth, sucked her lips, and pulled her even closer still. They were so close, so hot for each other, it felt like she was melting into him. Was this how it felt to truly become one with another person? If so, she wanted more. She wanted him.

A sob bubbled up inside of her when he pulled back, but then he lifted her arms and she felt the soft cotton of her shirt brush over her body as he pulled it up and off. Next, his fingers were gripping the waistband of her jeans and pulling her back to him, crashing her into the hard plane of his chest.

His mouth met hers again in an intense kiss, like he was a dying man drinking from her as if she was a tall glass of cold water. Ryleigh gasped when he gripped her ass, and pushed himself into her. He was hard, and the thought that she made him that way excited her even more.

Dazed and a little crazy, she pulled back, gasping for air before she gripped his head and tugged him back down to her waiting lips. He groaned when she bit down lightly on his bottom lip.

"Ryleigh, are you sure?"

She wanted to scream "yes." She wanted to push him down on the sofa and ride him until dawn. But the one word he needed to hear didn't come out. Nodding quickly, she placed his hand over her rapidly beating heart.

He took the opportunity to cup her breast in his hand. Sighing, he rested his forehead against hers. "I need to hear you say it."

"Please," she whimpered, letting her head fall back as he traced his tongue down her neck.

"Damn, you're so beautiful. Do you even realize how much I want you? I just want to hear you tell me that you want this as much as I do. Say it, Ryleigh." His low voice, the way he said her name, the heat of him against her, made her ache.

He slipped a hand inside her underwear, capturing her moan with another kiss. Every touch of his lips to hers, sent a shiver down her spine and made her tremble with need. It was so good, it hurt.

"Yes," she breathed finally.

"Yes, what," he murmured against her temple as he worked her with his fingers. She moved her hips in time with his movements, chasing the release that was building inside of her. "Ryleigh, say it. Tell me what you want."

"I can't...I can't concentrate."

"I can help you with that." He twisted his hand and hit that spot that made her knees feel weak.

Before she could brace for it, her orgasm tore through her. She screamed as it took her over for several sweet seconds. He wrapped his free arm around her like a steel band, right before her legs gave out. Martin kissed her chin before he bit down on it gently.

Her eyes fluttered open and she found him staring at her, amusement in his eyes.

"Better?" he asked.

Nodding, she chewed on her bottom lip. "Much."

"So..." he started moving his fingers, winding her up again. Her mouth fell open on a sigh. "Say it. What do you want?"

"You. Your hands, your mouth, you—" Her breath caught in her throat on the word she wanted to say when he brushed against her clit. "Inside me."

One minute, she was standing, blissfully close to another orgasm. The next, she was floating, as he lifted her over his shoulder and carried her through the house as if he owned it. She let out a loud "Whoop!" when he smacked her butt. Laughing, she smacked his ass for good measure.

"Which one is your room?"

She giggled, impressed that he was carrying her like she weighed only a few pounds. "End of the hall, on the right."

He stepped into her room, and set her down. He glanced around the room, and she tensed. Martin Sullivan not only made her laugh, melt, and come so hard she wanted to weep, he was now the only man who had ever seen her bedroom.

Suddenly self-conscious, she wondered what he was thinking as he took in her space, her sanctuary. *Thank God, I washed clothes.* Just to be sure, she stole a glance at the floor in front of her closet. She let out a sigh of relief at the empty clothes hamper.

"Take your pants off," he ordered softly.

"What if I want you to do it for me?"

He chuckled, shaking his head. "Now, Ryleigh. That's no fun." He stepped closer, placing his hands on her hips and turning her around. She watched him through the mirror on her dresser. Kissing her chin, he thrust his erection into her back. "Do it slow," he commanded.

She locked her gaze on his and followed his instructions, slowly pulling her jeans down. Bending low, she pushed her ass into his hard dick, enjoying the curse that slipped from his lips. His hands on her hips held her in that position and she rubbed against him. Straightening to her full height slowly, she met his hungry eyes in the mirror.

He hooked a finger in the waist of her underwear and snapped it lightly against her skin. She took that as a sign and removed her panties.

Once she was standing upright again, she took a moment to observe herself in the mirror. Ryleigh wasn't petite by any means; she had more than a few problem areas, but she'd never been self-conscious about her nakedness in front of men. She had Mama Lil to thank for that. But being there with him, in nothing but her bra, made her feel exposed. Not just naked, but bare. Open.

Ryleigh brushed her hand over her stomach and held it there, giving in to the urge to cover up a little.

Martin gripped her wrist. "Don't do that. Don't cover yourself." His fingers whispered over her stomach, and she trembled as he traced her belly button. "You're beautiful, Ryleigh."

She arched a brow. "And you have on too many clothes, Marty-Mar."

He laughed, and she grinned up at him, kissing his jaw. "You got jokes, huh?" Cupping her sex in his hand, he squeezed. Ryleigh gasped as he slid a finger over her slit and circled her clit. "Damn, Gina," he grumbled in her ear.

She felt him shake with laughter against her back, and she joined him. *Good one.* In Brazil, they'd both shared their love of the television show, *Martin.* That's when he'd mentioned that he'd grown tired of "Martin" jokes and people calling him "Marty-Mar" really quick. The phrase "Damn, Gina" was also one made popular from the show, and usually meant Martin's TV wife was getting on his nerves. *This is fun.* Ryleigh had never joked around with anyone prior to sex. It felt good, natural.

When their laughter subsided, she felt more comfortable, and allowed herself to relax against him. Reaching behind his shoulder, she pulled his shirt up and off, tossing it somewhere to her left. He pulled his belt off and dropped his jeans, kicking them to his right.

The corners of his mouth quirked into a grin. "Better?"

"Yes."

Martin pushed a strap of her bra off her shoulder, and trailed sweet kisses down her neck. Ryleigh pinched her leg, unable to believe this was happening. She was actually going to be with Martin again, in her bed.

Turning around, she brushed her lips over his, before she whispered against his ear, "Make love to me?"

MARTIN WASN'T sure when things had changed between them. It

just happened. He'd had every intention of going home. He wanted to end the night with a kiss and the promise of another night, another date. As usual, his common sense flew out the window at her soft plead for him to stay.

Things had taken on a life of their own, and he was helpless to stop the inevitable. That kiss in her living room, the striptease he'd demanded she give him, was everything. And now she'd asked him to make love to her.

Knowing Ryleigh, he was sure she hadn't meant it to come out as a question. She was a take-charge woman, and would most likely have wanted to assert a little control over the situation. But the crack in her voice and the vulnerable, almost innocent, look in her eyes when she'd pulled back to meet his gaze did him in.

Caressing her face, he grazed her lips with his, breathing her in. The intoxicating scent of her soft perfume, wafted to his nose. He wanted to taste every inch of her skin, hear her whisper his name over and over again.

He traced his tongue over her collarbone and took one breast in his mouth, circling the nipple with his tongue. She dug her fingernails into his arms as he kissed his way over to her other breast and paid it the same attention. From there, he kissed the underside of each breast, and down her quivering stomach, dipping his tongue into her navel.

Dropping down to his knees, he placed tiny, wet kisses on her upper thighs and nudged her legs open. Rubbing the backs of her legs, he brushed his lips over her inner thighs before licking her core, dipping his tongue inside her and sucking her clit into his mouth. She braced one hand on his shoulder and held his head there with the other one, parting her legs wider as he feasted on her, tasted her sweetness. Never before had he wanted to spend time worshipping someone, finding the spots on her body that made her sing with pleasure. It didn't take long for her to climax, wildly undulating her hips as she came.

When she sagged against the dresser, sated, he stood to his full height and kissed her. They groaned in unison as their mouths met.

"Condom?" he grumbled, burying his face in her neck and placing a gentle bite on the sensitive skin there.

She fumbled with the drawer behind her. A frenzy seemed to overtake him and he yanked the drawer out, pulling it off the tracks.

They both looked down at the drawer, which was now hanging low. "Shit," he mumbled. "Did I break it?"

She pulled him back in for a kiss. "I don't care," she muttered against his mouth, tracing his lips with her tongue before she dipped it into his mouth.

Groaning, he felt around the bottom of the drawer for a condom. Soon the tips of his fingers brushed over plastic and he picked up the small package and tore it open, never breaking the kiss. He slid on the condom and whirled her around, turning her to face the mirror again.

Martin couldn't take his eyes off her body, those full hips, her soft skin, her breasts. He glanced at her face, which was flushed red from her neck to her ears. Her hooded eyes stared back at him. She bit down on her lip and he swiped his thumb over it. "Stop. Mine."

"What's yours?"

"Your lips." He lowered his head, kissed her, keeping one eye on their reflection. If it was possible, he hardened more at the sight of them in sync. "Mine," he repeated as he gripped her hips in his hand.

"Martin," she whispered, leaning forward.

"I want you to watch me take you this way." He needed her to see how she looked when she came. And hoped she realized how glorious she was when she truly let go.

He pushed into her with one movement, loving her sharp intake of breath as he filled her completely. Pulling her up against him so he could see her body, he was unable to tear his gaze away from the way he looked inside her. He swept his hands over her soft skin, tracing invisible circles over her.

Ryleigh's body called to him, whispered to him to move, to take her. But he wanted her to tell him what she wanted him to do. Martin had taken charge of the foreplay, made sure she was ready and open for him, but now this was her show. He was big and didn't want to take it too fast. But she was so wet, so tight... Her comfort was more important than his need at that moment, and he wanted to let her set the pace. "How do you want it?"

"I want it hard," she whispered.

Thrusting forward, Martin closed his eyes when a whimper escaped her swollen mouth. He sent up a silent prayer of thanks at her soft command because he knew he wouldn't last much longer.

But when she pushed her ass back against him and told him it was okay, his thin control snapped. He pumped into her hard and fast. She met him with a fire of her own. He could tell she wanted this as much as he did, and he let that propel him forward. Her orgasm was fierce and quick. He felt it before he heard her groan his name again and again. Her reaction and the feel of her release was enough to send him over the edge.

Nearly two hours later, after Martin had scooped Ryleigh up and carried her over to the bed and made love to her again, the two lay tangled up in her massive bed.

"What are you thinking about?" Ryleigh asked, entwining her fingers with his.

How much I could get used to this. He didn't say it out loud, though. It wasn't the right time. If possible, their lovemaking this time was even better. The sultry backdrop of Brazil had nothing on the sincere connection they'd just shared.

"Martin?" she asked, perching herself up on her elbow and looking down at him. "Are you okay?"

Uncertainty clouded her eyes, and he leaned forward to place a kiss on her brow. "I'm good."

She relaxed onto him again. "Are you going to tell me what you're thinking about?"

"I want you again."

It wasn't a lie. It was very much the truth. Martin knew he wouldn't be able to get enough of her. Unfortunately, he was a little leery. *Will she kick me out?*

Ryleigh giggled. "You're insatiable."

"You're—" *Mine.* "—gorgeous when you come with my name on your lips."

"Oh God, you make me crazy."

"Hopefully, in a good way."

She turned, bringing her leg over his. He squeezed her thigh. "A very good way." She leaned in to kiss him, and his stomach growled. Laughing, she said, "Someone worked up an appetite."

Martin watched her slide off the bed and slip on his T-shirt. Turning to him, she winked.

"I like you in my shirt," he said, grabbing a hold of the hem of the shirt and tugging her forward. "Now, take it off and get back in the bed."

"No, silly. Come on." She held her hand out, and he took it reluctantly. "I'm going to fix you something to eat."

An hour later, Martin was sated and sleepy. *This woman is amazing.* As if he wasn't already enamored, Ryleigh had gone and cooked for him. And not just anything. The woman sitting across from him eating had asked him what he had a taste for, and when he'd told her pasta, she'd whipped up chicken with homemade alfredo sauce and spinach. And it was the best fettuccini alfredo he'd ever had.

"Damn, doll. You put your foot in that." He sat back in his chair. "Let me guess, Mama Lil taught you to cook?"

She nodded. "Yes, she did. Some things. But I love to cook, so I taught myself a few recipes as well. Right now, I can say that my chicken alfredo and my macaroni and cheese could beat hers in a contest. The only thing I haven't mastered is the grill."

I can handle that. The thought stunned him silent. Now, he was thinking about dinners with her where she cooked the sides and he grilled the meat?

She rose from her seat and took his plate. "I feel like you know all this stuff about me, but I don't know much about you."

"What do you want to know?"

Ryleigh rinsed off the plates and loaded them into the dishwasher. Then, she went about putting the food up and cleaning up the stove and countertops. "I don't know. Have you always loved to work with computers?"

"Actually, yes. They've always fascinated me."

"Not everyone is lucky enough to get it right on their first try. What else do you like to do?"

Martin realized this type of conversation should have probably taken place before they'd slept together, but he went with it. "I learned how to hack computers when I was a teenager."

She whirled around from her spot at the sink, her mouth open. "Really?"

"Yes. But I quickly learned that could get me into serious trouble."

Ryleigh wiped her hands and joined him at the table again. "I bet. Did you get arrested or something?"

"Actually, I accidentally discovered my coach's wife had been cheating on him. I told him and all hell broke loose. My father threatened me to stop meddling in people's affairs and took away my car for a whole year."

"You'd think he'd be happy you found out the truth and told someone. Saved your coach a lot of trouble."

"Except he was married to my aunt, my dad's sister. But I loved my football coach more than my aunt. She was mean as hell and Coach was like a second father to me. I was livid on his behalf."

"Yikes. So, yeah, I can see why your father was mad. But you did the right thing."

Martin thought about his Aunt Leila. She'd still never forgiven him for breaking up her marriage, even though she was the one in the wrong. They hadn't spoken to each other since the incident, over fifteen years ago.

"What made you go into business for yourself?" she asked.

"I met my business partner, Carter, in college. We were room-mates. Both of us wanted to do something different with our skills, and kind of fell into it after working for huge corporations after graduation."

Ryleigh nodded. "Your parents? Are they happy with your career choices?"

"My parents have always been supportive."

"Do you see them a lot?"

"I'm their only child. I try to get down to Texas to visit several times a year."

Martin's father, Sheldon, was a Vice President in R&D at Texas Instruments. And his mother, Lynne, was a Nurse Manager at Baylor University Medical Center. His extended family were spread out all over the United States.

"Why Michigan?" she asked.

Martin had decided early on that he wanted to play football at University of Michigan in Ann Arbor. The school offered him a scholarship to play ball. He played for his full college career, and then decided that he didn't want to try and play professionally. Instead, he enrolled in a graduate program and entered the workforce.

"I still can't believe you're a hacker." She crossed her arms over her chest.

"Not anymore. Well, not really."

She stood up and stretched. "I think I'm going to jump in the shower."

Well, it was good while it lasted.

Ryleigh walked to the doorway leading back to her bedroom, then turned on her heels and pulled off his shirt. "Care to join me?"

7

Life had a strange way of coming full circle. Ryleigh had spent the last several weeks hanging out with Martin, and she'd enjoyed every last minute with him. Things had quickly escalated between them after their first date. Chuckling to herself, Ryleigh still couldn't believe she'd made him chicken alfredo at three o'clock in the morning.

Since that night, she'd cooked for him many times, and he'd even grilled for her. They spent hours talking on the phone when he was out of town on business, learning about each other. Ryleigh never grew tired of talking to him or sleeping with him or eating with him or just being with him.

Waking up with him in the morning was fast becoming one of her favorite things to do, too. It was ironic considering their Brazil history. Although he traveled throughout the week, he made sure he spent his free nights with her, and she couldn't be happier.

Aside from the occasional text or call, she'd barely talked to anyone. Except for her daily calls with Mama Lil, who was still being her evasive self. Ava had called a few times to tell her how married life was treating her, but they didn't talk about Martin.

She hadn't shared this new development with any of her girls, which made her feel like she was hiding something from them.

The monthly conference call was on this month, so she planned to tell them about her and Martin then. They hadn't defined their relationship yet, but she was pretty sure he considered her his girlfriend. Especially since, he'd invited her home to Texas with him for Thanksgiving.

Love hadn't entered the equation yet, but Ryleigh was sure she was in love with him. The thought had scared her on many occasions and she'd often considered breaking things off before she was in too deep. But she couldn't bring herself to do it. Things were so good, though, that she wondered when the other shoe would drop. It always did for her. However, she purposed within herself to just enjoy it while it lasted.

Her cell phone rang, and she glanced down at it. The number wasn't familiar, but the area code was a South Carolina one, so she picked up. "Ryleigh Fields."

"Ms. Fields?" the female voice called over the receiver.

"Yes?"

"My name is Amy. I'm a charge nurse at the Rosewood Heights Health Center. Lillian Roberts named you as her emergency contact."

Ryleigh's stomach fell. *Mama Lil.* "I am. Is she okay?"

"She wanted me to call you," the nurse explained. "Are you available to talk?"

Ryleigh stood, walked over to her office door, and closed it. "Yes, is she okay?" she asked again.

"Yes, she's here for a follow-up appointment. I'm going to put you on speakerphone, okay?" Ryleigh heard shuffling, then she heard the nurse call out. "Ms. Fields, I have Ms. Roberts in the office with me."

"Ry-girl?" she heard Mama Lil say.

Ryleigh clutched her phone to her ear. "Yes, Mama Lil. I'm here. What's going on?"

"Ms. Fields," the nurse said. "Lillian came in for a routine mammogram a few weeks ago." *Oh God, no.* Ryleigh knew what was coming next, but she could hardly swallow, let alone articulate anything verbally. "The mammogram showed a lump in her right breast. A subsequent needle biopsy indicated there is cancer."

Tears welled up in Ryleigh's eyes and she let them fall freely. "Uh." She cleared her throat, willing herself to get it together. For Mama Lil. "What does this mean? Do you know what stage it is?"

"It's Stage Ia."

Ryleigh unlocked her laptop and typed in a search for breast cancer staging. Several articles popped up and she clicked on the Susan G. Komen link. As the nurse explained Mama Lil's diagnosis and treatment options, Ryleigh skimmed the article, jotting down several questions.

"Ms. Roberts has elected to do the surgical biopsy, or lumpectomy," the nurse said. "Followed by a course of radiation. It's good that she has never missed a mammogram. We got it early. There's no reason to believe she won't go on from this and live a long time."

"Thank you for calling me," Ryleigh said. "Can I talk to Mama Lil?"

Mama Lil had been suspiciously quiet during the conversation and that concerned Ryleigh.

"Sure," the kind nurse said.

A few seconds later, Mama Lil's voice came through the receiver. "Ry-girl? I'm okay."

Ryleigh wanted to reach through the phone and choke Mama Lil for keeping this from her. More than that, though, she wanted to just hug her. "Are you? You know, I thought we agreed you would tell me if something was wrong with you. I could have been there with you."

"I'm telling you now."

"After the mammogram, the needle aspiration, and the staging. Mama Lil, I need you to be okay. If something happened to you, I—"

"Girl, please. I'm going to be just fine. I just couldn't bring myself to tell you. So my friend, Amy, said that she would. I meet with the surgeon and my oncologist next week."

"Is this your way of telling me to come to Rosewood Heights?"

Silence.

"Mama Lil?"

"Yes," Mama Lil answered, her voice shaky. "If you can spare the time, I'd like you to be here."

Ryleigh knew it took a lot for Mama Lil to admit she needed anything. She wouldn't disappoint her and not be there. Especially since Mama Lil had always been there for her.

She wanted to break down, rail against the world for always dropping that other shoe. It wasn't too much to ask to be happy, for once. She'd been through hell as a child, didn't even know how she would make it through the night sometimes. It was Mama Lil that had made her life better, showed her the love she so desperately needed.

"I'll be there," Ryleigh promised. "I'm booking the first flight out."

"No need to rush, Ry-girl."

"Yes, there is. You need someone. And I'm going to take care of you, just like you've always taken care of me. No arguing. I'll be there as soon as possible."

Ryleigh spoke with the nurse and Mama Lil for a few more minutes before disconnecting the call. Her day was shot. She was supposed to meet Martin at his place later. Now, she had to book a flight back home. She considered calling him, to let him know what was going on. But she suspected that hearing his voice would cause the dam to break. So, instead, she would concentrate on making the necessary arrangements.

I can't fall apart. Not when Mama Lil needed her most. She had to be on her game when talking to the doctors, when making sure that the restaurant was running efficiently, when talking to Mama Lil. There was so much to do. First, she needed to talk to her boss.

It took a minute to get in with her boss, but she managed to see him between meetings. Once she'd explained the situation to him, he'd been very understanding and agreed to let her work remotely during the time she needed to be in Rosewood Heights. The rest of her afternoon was spent working with IT to make sure her laptop was outfitted with the correct software.

Once she arrived at her house, she started packing. She hadn't spoken with Martin all day, and it was for the best. She needed to make sure everything was taken care of before she lost herself in him.

But there was one call she wanted to make. She sent out the necessary nine-one-one texts.

The first call came from Ava. "Ry, what's wrong?"

Ryleigh preferred to tell everyone at once. "I'll explain everything once everyone is on the line."

They spent a few minutes conferencing in the rest of the ladies. It had been a while, so they took some time to catch up, letting each other know briefly what their month had been like. Mac had shared the funny story of her new and unexpected love connection with the best man at the wedding, Alex. Quinn waxed poetic about the beauty of love and Raven managed to keep the conversation geared to anyone but herself.

"Ava, how was the honeymoon?" Quinn asked

Ava described the paradise she and Owen escaped to for two weeks. The two were blissfully happy, and had started talking about babies. Already.

"Don't you think it's a little early?" Raven asked. "You just started having sex. Enjoy it."

Ryleigh laughed, grateful that she'd called in the reinforcements. This call was exactly what she needed to keep her mind off of everything. Inevitably, she knew her friends would turn their attention to her, but she enjoyed hearing about all of their lives.

It was Ava who broke the ice. "Ry, you asked for this emergency call. Spill."

"Yeah, Ry," Mac said. "Tell us what's going on. Does this have anything to do with Mr. Trouble with the impressive dick attached?"

Ryleigh burst out into a fit of laughter. It was just like Mac to bring up something she'd texted her on a whim. When she'd initially had the thought, the first and only person she'd thought to tell was Mac. Shit, she needed to get it out. Martin had been giving her the flux at the time.

"Wait a minute, who is this guy?" Ava asked.

"Aw, come on now," Raven said. "You're holding out."

"Ryleigh, you are so nasty," Quinn added with a laugh.

"Okay, okay." Ryleigh sighed. "I guess there are a lot of things to talk about. His name is Martin."

"Wait, Owen's cousin?" Ava asked.

"Yes." Ryleigh gave a brief history on her past and present with Martin. "Ladies, he's wonderful. I've never been with anyone like him. I mean, I cooked dinner for him in the middle of the night after he gave me some of that impressive—"

"Stop!" Quinn shouted. "We got the picture."

Ryleigh continued, telling them all about Martin. "I think I love him."

Silence. And it was like that for what seemed like eternity.

"Hello?" Ry said, irritation flaring within her. "I tell you that I think I love someone and all I get is silence?"

The first scream came from Quinn, followed by an "oh shit" from Mac. Ava and Raven were a little more reserved with their responses, but all of them were genuinely happy for her. Now, for the bad news.

"And Mama Lil is sick," Ryleigh announced.

More silence.

Ryleigh figured the ladies were waiting for her to continue, so she did. "It's breast cancer, stage 1a. They're doing a lumpectomy soon. So, I'm flying down to Rosewood Heights tonight."

"Aw damn, Ry," Mac said. "I'm so sorry to hear this. I love Mama Lil."

I do, too. "I know. She's been a part of our lives for years. She's scared. Hell, I'm scared. But I'm glad they caught it before it spread to another organ."

"Do you need somewhere to stay, Ry?" Ava asked. "You can stay at Prescott Manor. My parents are out of the country for a few months on vacation."

Ryleigh appreciated the support her friends always provided. That is why they would always be her "sisters." Mama Lil had once told her "family is not always tied by blood." That couldn't be more true.

The rest of the call was understandably more somber. But Ryleigh still loved hearing their voices. Eventually, she glanced at her watch. *Shit.* She was late as hell. Martin would be expecting her. She told her friends that she'd be in touch with updates about Mama Lil and ended the call.

Ava called right back, asking for her flight information. They chatted for a few minutes, and Ava arranged for a rental car so that Ryleigh could drive to her parents' home and not rely on a cab or shuttle. Once they'd confirmed the arrangements, Ava assured her she'd check on Mama Lil that night before hanging up.

Sighing, Ryleigh finished packing. When she was done, she glanced around her condo one last time, locked up, and left.

RYLEIGH WAS LATE. And it wasn't like her. Martin busied himself cleaning up his already clean house. He'd just returned from Phoenix and couldn't wait to see her. He'd missed her.

Martin knew he was in love with Ryleigh. It had snuck up on him right around the time she breezed back into his life at his cousin's wedding. He'd never pegged himself to be "that guy" but *it is what it is*. He'd fallen hard for the beauty with the big brown eyes, and the even bigger heart. There were so many times she could have let her life and her circumstances keep her from doing anything. Her resilience made him love her more.

He hoped that his declaration wouldn't send her running for the hills. They'd come a long way, after all. He'd spent several nights and mornings with her in the weeks since their first date.

The last time he was home, he'd introduced her to Aisha. The two women had hit it off, which was huge considering Aisha had never cared for any woman he'd dated. In fact, Ryleigh and Aisha had recently scheduled a spa day, and had already spent several hundred dollars shopping together.

When Martin had introduced Ryleigh to Carter, his partner was sold immediately. It could have been the breakfast she'd cooked, though. Carter had surprised him one morning and showed up at his place intent on going to the gym to shoot some ball. Unfortunately, he'd caught Martin with his pants unzipped. Literally.

Ryleigh had immediately put his embarrassed best friend at ease, offering to feed him. The two—his brother and his girl—had bonded over scrambled eggs. Carter had insisted that no one could scramble an egg like his mother. Well, Ryleigh proved to be a worthy opponent for Mrs. Iris Johnston. Since then, every time he talked to Carter, his friend asked if he was treating Ryleigh well.

A knock at his door jarred him from his thoughts. He hurried to answer. When he opened the door, Ryleigh was standing there, her head down. "Doll?" She looked up at him then, her chin quivering. He pulled her to him and hugged her.

He held her like that for a moment, letting her cry into his shirt. Eventually, her sobs subsided and she pulled away. He brushed a thumb under her eye.

"Mama Lil is sick." Ryleigh walked past him into his home, kicking off her shoes.

Frowning, he closed the door and followed her into the den. "What?"

She sat down on his favorite chair, and tucked her legs underneath her. He took a seat in front of her on the coffee table. "She has breast cancer."

Martin rubbed her knee, then gave it a little squeeze. "Oh wow. How is she handling it?"

Her worried eyes met his, and his heart squeezed in his chest. "She wants me to come there. She's scared, and I want to be there for her."

Martin understood that, and expected nothing less. "As you should be. What are the doctors saying?"

"It's curable. They expect her to make a full recovery."

"That's good." He titled his head, met her gaze. "My mother works with breast cancer survivors. If it's caught early enough, treatment options are better."

"Yeah, I know. I did some research when she told me. It's the treatment that worries me. She has to have surgery to remove the lump, then radiation. From everything I've read, it's the radiation that will be hard. She has a business to run, and people are depending on her."

"Well, she has you to help her out." He stretched forward, brushed a finger down the ridge of her nose. "And you'll do what you have to do. When do you leave?"

She chewed on her bottom lip, and like always, he rubbed his thumb over it, freeing it from her teeth. "Tonight. I leave tonight."

Damn. That was fast. He hated that he was disappointed, even though he knew she had to go. "Oh. What time is your flight?" He glanced at his watch.

"I have to be at the airport at nine o'clock. My flight leaves at eleven."

"I'm taking you to the airport." There was no way he was letting her walk out of here without him. He couldn't fly with her that night, but he had no intention of staying away, or leaving her to deal with this alone. In his mind, he'd already started making plans, thinking about meetings he could push out and clients that would be okay dealing with him remotely instead of in person.

She gave him a wobbly smile. "Thank you. I'm sorry. I know you had plans for us."

"Doll, please. This is more important. Mama Lil is your family, and family comes first. You want to eat? I love you."

Ryleigh's eyes widened. "Huh? What did you just say?"

What the hell *did* he just say? Shaking his head, he cursed inwardly. "I didn't mean to say it like that." He stood, paced the

ELLE WRIGHT

floor several times, before stopping in front of her. He held out a hand, and she took it, letting him pull her to her feet.

"So, you don't love me?"

"No, I do love you. I just wanted to say it differently." Ryleigh stepped into him, wrapping her arms around his waist. "I think it was perfect."

He bent lower, leaned his forehead against hers. "Perfect, huh? Perfect and lame as hell."

She laughed, and he couldn't help the smile that tugged at his own lips. "Stop, Martin. It wasn't lame. You're not lame. I love you, too."

Martin cupped her face in his hands, searched her eyes. "I'm not sure I expected you to say it back, but I'm glad you did."

RYLEIGH LIFTED HERSELF UP, kissing Martin with everything she had. He'd said he wasn't planning to tell her that he loved her the way he did, but she wasn't sorry. It was as unpredictable as everything else about their relationship.

"Make love to me," she whispered against his ear before biting down on it gently. "Now."

He lifted her in his arms, and she wrapped her legs around his lean waist. As he carried her into his bedroom, he kissed her tenderly, drawing a low moan from her belly. In two-point-two seconds, she was ready, her core already wet and quivering with want.

Lying her down on her back, he took his time stripping her clothes off, teasing her until she was trembling with need. Her body was alive, tingling from his touch. She'd nearly come undone as he coaxed her legs open and nuzzled against her warm center. And that was with her panties on.

Naked now, she raised her arms, beckoning him to come to her. He made quick work of taking his own clothes off, then rested between her legs. She wrapped her legs around him, squeezing him to her.

"I love you," he whispered against her mouth, as he entered her. "So much."

"I love you, too."

Instead of hard and fast like she liked it, he took his time, stroking her so slow she felt him everywhere from the soles of her feet to the crown of her head. Their leisurely pace seemed to shine a spotlight on how much she needed him, making her want to hold on even tighter to him.

After all these years, she could finally imagine sharing her life with someone, loving someone and being loved in return. Martin had not only told her he loved her, he was proving that he did with his actions. The simple action of understanding and acceptance had changed her life. Because he did accept her, all of her. Flaws and all.

As they made love to each other, pleasure coiled low in her belly, making her arch her back up off the bed. She kissed every inch of his skin that she could reach before pulling him into a kiss. "I need you," she whispered. "Martin, I need this."

He finally picked up his pace, pushing into her harder and faster. "Let go for me, doll. I got you."

His words were enough. Ryleigh fell over the cliff, coming so long and hard she saw stars. Then, he was there kissing her back down to earth.

Martin smiled down at Ryleigh, and she couldn't help but grin up at him. "I'm sleepy."

"Sleep, doll. I'll make sure you get up on time."

He rolled over on his back, pulling her with him. She burrowed against his side and let sleep take her.

Ryleigh woke up with a start, reaching blindly for her phone.

"It's okay. You have some time," Martin said, rubbing her back.

She let out a deep breath, and then turned toward him. He was lying on his back, the sheet draped low on his waist. "What time is it?" She rubbed her hair.

"It's eight."

Ryleigh rested against his chest. "I'd better get a shower."

She didn't want to leave him. She wasn't sure when she'd get to see him again. He was a business owner and had to travel for work, so she didn't expect him to drop everything and fly to freakin' Rosewood Heights with her. But that didn't stop her from wanting him to do just that, though.

8

———

Ryleigh stared down at Mama Lil's still body. The surgery had been a success, pretty routine. She didn't even have to stay the night in the hospital, which made both of them feel better. Stroking Lil's arm, Ryleigh noted the warmth there. She took comfort in the feel of her soft skin under her fingertips.

According to the doctors, Mama Lil should wake up soon. Ryleigh couldn't wait to see her, to talk to her. She'd been in Rosewood Heights for two weeks. It had been good to just spend time with Mama Lil, time when she wasn't rushing to catch the next flight or handling wedding party responsibilities, or even putting out some stupid fire that her mother caused.

It had just been her and Mama Lil. Her "Mama" had insisted she help at the restaurant in the days leading up to the surgery, and Ryleigh had been happy to be there. It gave her an opportunity to see how things worked and get to know the new employees a little better.

Martin had called every day to check on her, making sure she ate and drank enough water because he knew she had a tendency to forget to hydrate. That morning, in fact, he'd asked to speak to

Mama Lil and the two of them had talked in hushed tones for a few minutes before Mama Lil gave her the phone back.

When she'd asked Martin what he'd said, his answer was a resounding, "None of your business."

He's been talking to her too much. Martin and Mama Lil had formed quite the bond. The two were thick as thieves. It didn't irritate her as much as she assumed it would. It only strengthened her feelings for him. Any man she was with would have to love and respect Mama Lil.

Mama Lil's eyes fluttered open finally, and she whispered something.

Ryleigh inched closer, straining to hear the words tumbling out of Mama Lil's mouth. "Hey." She squeezed Mama's shoulder. "I'm here."

"Ry-girl." The older woman's voice was raspy, weak.

"It's me."

Mama Lil motioned to her throat, and Ryleigh wet her mouth with a swab stick that was ready and waiting in a cup of water. "What did the doctor say?" she asked once she cleared her throat.

"The surgery went well. They removed the tumor, got everything. The surgeon will be in to talk with you soon."

Mama Lil nodded, swallowing visibly and wincing as if it had caused her pain. "I love you, Ry-girl."

Emotion clogged Ryleigh's throat. "I love you, too."

"That man. Martin? He loves you, too."

She squeezed Mama Lil's hand. "I know, Mama."

"I'm glad you found him," she croaked. Ryleigh wet her mouth again with a swab. "He's a good man."

Ryleigh knew Martin was a good man, a loyal man, a trustworthy man. "He likes you, too."

"Who said anything about liking him?"

Laughing, Ryleigh rubbed the hair from Mama Lil's forehead. "You're a mess. Remember when I told you that you were like the grandmother I never had?"

Mama Lil rolled her eyes and groaned. "And I told you I'm not old enough to be your grandma," she grumbled.

Ryleigh giggled, remembering the conversation they'd just had one day earlier. "Well, I was wrong."

Mama Lil opened one eye, a frown creasing the lines of her forehead.

"Mama Lil, you were like the mother I never had." Ryleigh meant every word she'd just uttered. Her mother wasn't a mother to her, and Mama Lil had stepped in without even being asked. She'd sowed the seed in Ryleigh's life that had helped her grow and fly.

A tear fell from Mama Lil's eye and Ryleigh used a piece of Kleenex to dab the corner of her eye.

"Now, you done made me cry," Mama Lil said. "You owe me an apology."

Ryleigh barked out a laugh. "I'm not sorry." She leaned down and gave her a peck on the cheek. "Rest. I'll be here when you wake up."

Soon, Mama Lil was asleep again.

Ryleigh plopped down in the reclining chair. *Thank God.* She could breathe a little easier now. Mama Lil was going to be alright.

"Knock, knock."

Ryleigh looked up to see Ava standing in the doorway, a bouquet of flowers in her hand. "Hey."

Ava breezed in the room, ever the professional in a pinstriped pantsuit and leather ankle boots. "I figured I'd drop by and check on you." She held up a bag. "I brought you food and water. You need to eat something."

Ryleigh feigned offense. "How do you know I didn't eat?"

Ava shot her a look that told her the answer to that question. "Please, I know you, girl. You never eat when you're supposed to." She set the bag in Ryleigh's lap. "Eat."

Following orders, Ryleigh pulled a huge, warm blueberry muffin from the bag. Ryleigh bit into a piece, and closed her eyes.

Roseberry Bakery was just what the doctor ordered. The warm blueberry muffin hit the spot.

"And I also stopped by the restaurant to check on the employees," Ava continued as she organized the flowers and cards from the townspeople on the window sill. "Everything looks good. The staff is worried, so I told them either me or you would call. Also, the girls have been texting all morning. I told them I'd send an update soon."

Ryleigh nodded, swallowing a big bite of her muffin, then taking a gulp of water. "Thanks for everything, Ava. I really appreciate it."

"Girl, no need to thank me. You're my sister. Period. I'm always here for you."

Ryleigh had been overwhelmed by the support she'd received from not only her friends, but the people in town. It didn't feel like she was Harriet Field's daughter anymore. She felt like she was Lillian Robert's daughter.

"Have you talked to Martin today?" Ava asked, a smile on her face.

Frowning, Ryleigh glanced at her phone to see if he'd called. "Earlier. But not in a few hours."

Wiping her hands, she picked up her phone and dialed Martin. He answered on the first ring. "Hey, doll. How are you?"

"Hey, baby. I'm okay. Missing you."

"I miss you, too." She heard him say something to a woman in the background. The woman said something in response, but Ryleigh couldn't make it out. Martin told the woman, "Thanks. I got it from here."

Curious, Ryleigh asked, "Where are you?"

"On my way to handle something very important."

"For business?"

"Not really. How's Mama Lil?"

Ryleigh glanced over at Mama Lil. "She's sleeping. The surgeon said everything went well. They didn't see any other signs of cancer, so that's great. She woke for a little bit. Still funny as ever."

"Are you alone?" It sounded like he was walking.

"Ava's here chilling with me a minute."

She could hear rustling on the other line, and the ding of something in the background, like an elevator. "Good."

"If you're busy, you can call me back."

"Doll, I'm never too busy for you."

She leaned back in the chair, a smile on her face. "I love you."

"I love you, too. Are you eating?"

Ryleigh tapped her foot against the tile, looked at her nails. *I need a manicure.* "Yes, Martin. I ate."

"Hope you enjoyed that muffin Ava brought you."

She froze. *How does he know Ava brought me a muffin?* She locked her gaze on Ava's. Her best friend had a goofy grin on her face. "Wait. Martin, how did you know I had a muffin? Did Ava call you?"

"No, I called Ava. She is married to my cousin, ya know?"

Still confused, she asked, "Where are you?"

"Right here, wondering why you haven't finished your muffin. That shit was not cheap."

Her eyes flashed to the door. Martin was standing there, looking all fine, with the phone against his ear.

"You're here," she said into the phone.

"You can hang up the phone now." He dropped his into his pocket.

Jerking her phone away from her ear, she whispered, "Oh my God."

"Are you just going to sit there and stare at me?"

Ryleigh jumped out of her seat and ran into his waiting arms, holding on for dear life.

———

MARTIN HELD RYLEIGH, and winked at Ava who waved at him. She and Owen had picked him up from the airport and drove him into town. He'd stopped on the way to get the muffin and Ava convinced him to let her go in first so she could actually see the surprise in Ryleigh's face when he surprised her.

For his part, he didn't care how it happened. He just wanted to see his girl. All of his plans circled the drain when one of their primary client's systems went down, so he'd been forced to cancel his initial flight.

According to Ryleigh and Ava, the time with Mama Lil had been good for her, so he couldn't regret that.

He kissed her temple, and leaned back to get a look at her face. "I told you to eat. I figured I'd buy you one of those blueberry muffins you like to rave about. Mrs. Oak said she'd just pulled it out of the oven."

She peered up at him with shiny eyes, and pulled her back to him. "Oh, shut up." She nuzzled her nose into his neck.

Martin brushed his fingers over the back of her head. "Look at me, doll."

"I can't," she mumbled.

"Yes, you can."

She finally stepped back, wiping her eyes. "I don't know why I'm so emotional."

He didn't know, either. But an emotional Ryleigh had made his protective instinct swell. He'd fight anybody, do anything, to protect her. "You're just stressed."

Martin kissed her brow, lingering there for a moment before turning his attention to her mouth. It was so ready, so ripe, for his kiss. Leaning down, he brushed his lips over the corners of her mouth before kissing her fully.

Suddenly, he heard a throat clear behind him, causing him to break the kiss. Glancing back, he glared at Owen. "Get the hell out of here." Owen cracked up laughing and strode over to Ava before sitting down on an empty chair next to her.

Martin took the seat Ryleigh vacated earlier and pulled her down on his lap. "You okay?"

She smiled. "I am now."

"I guess this means you missed me for real, huh?"

Nudging him, she grumbled, "If I weren't here in this hospital, I'd show you how much."

Visions of her sucking him off, crossed his mind. "You can show me later. I'm definitely interested in knowing how much you missed me."

"I can't believe you're here. I didn't think you were coming."

"I would have been here sooner," he explained, "but we had an client issue that I needed to handle."

"Well, it's the nature of the business you're in. I was okay, though."

"I know you're okay, but I wanted to be here with you."

"You guys are so damn corny," Owen said.

"I know, honey," Ava chimed in. "I can't believe Ryleigh is being all mushy. This is so unlike her. I can't wait to tell the girls."

"Shut up," Ryleigh said. "Leave us alone."

"You heard the woman," Martin agreed before turning his attention back to Ryleigh. "I heard about your little toast at the wedding."

Ryleigh's mouth fell open. "Wha-Who-Oh no. Who told you?" Her gaze shot back to Ava's. "Ava! How could you?"

Ava smacked Owen on the arm. "You told him?" Ava screeched. "I told you to keep it between us. Ugh."

Owen shrugged. "I didn't tell him."

"I'm so never telling you anything again." Ava shot his cousin a side eye. "I'm sorry, Ryleigh."

"It's okay, Ava," Martin said, deciding to fess up and let his cousin off the hook. "He didn't tell me. I promise."

Ryleigh felt her face flush. "Tell me who told you."

"Tell *me*...who were you planning to marry?" Martin asked.

"No one," Ryleigh grumbled. "I wasn't even dating anyone then. None of us were. It was just a silly toast." She paused a moment before saying, "Tell me who told you."

Motioning toward a sleeping Mama Lil, he said, "She told me this morning; said that I needed to come correct when the time comes."

He'd had a pretty enlightening phone conversation with Mama Lil that morning, before her surgery. The older woman had told him all about the drunken Best Friend's Challenge to get married before Ava and Owen's first wedding anniversary.

Martin got a kick out of the story, not because of crazy wedding pact, but because of the way Mama Lil told it. She was as colorful and as dramatic as his own Granny. He figured they'd get along just fine.

There was no doubt in his mind that the toast was a precursor of things to come. He'd already started shopping for rings, and he'd even brought his mother into it. His parents couldn't wait to meet Ryleigh.

Ryleigh's head came down on his chest. "I'm so embarrassed."

"It's okay." He pinched her chin. "I think it's cute. And accurate because we will be married by the end of the year."

Later on, Martin sat near Mama Lil's hospital bed, working on his laptop. The doctor had recommended Mama Lil stay overnight as opposed to leaving, so they'd decided to stay with her. Ryleigh lay stretched out on a reclining chair. It had been a long ass day, but he was glad to be with her and happy to be able to spend time with Owen and Ava that evening.

Mama Lil had been resting peacefully for the last several hours. He watched the older woman, wondered when he'd get a chance to really talk to her. Earlier, he'd told Ryleigh they'd be married by Spring. He intended to follow through with that promise. But he needed to get all of his ducks in a row, starting with getting official approval from the woman that Ryleigh considered her "mother."

"You're here." Mama Lil's voice was soft, but strong. Despite being laid up in the hospital, she still commanded the room.

"Yes, ma'am," he answered.

Mama Lil coughed, and he stood and handed her a cup of water that sat on the bedside tray. The older woman sipped carefully, before pushing the cup away. "Good." She cleared her throat. "She needs you."

"The feeling's mutual."

Mama Lil's eyes softened as she searched his. "You do love her, don't you?"

"I told you I did." He smiled when she rolled her eyes and swatted a hand in the air as if dismissing him.

When her watery gaze met his again, she gave him a tentative smile. "She's wounded. There's a part of her that is still that little girl looking for her mother's approval, despite what she says to the contrary."

Martin nodded, listening intently at Mama Lil. Ryleigh rarely talked about her mother. Actually, she didn't talk about her at all. Not since she'd told him about how she was conceived weeks ago.

Taking his seat again, he said, "She doesn't say much about her mother. I don't push her."

"When I met Ry-girl, she was broken. It took everything in me not to whoop Harriet's ass up and down the street for treating that beautiful girl the way she did."

Martin clenched his teeth together, fury rising in his bones at the thought of a scared Ryleigh. "Why didn't you?"

"Because she loved her mother. In spite of her denials, she didn't want her hurt. So I stood down for her. I've spent every day since then protecting her. Ryleigh is my daughter in every way that counts. And I need her to be okay. If she's not okay, I'm not okay."

Martin understood Mama Lil's words more than he could say. Glancing over at Ryleigh, he said, "She's okay. I'll do anything to make sure she is." Then, he met Mama Lil's gaze, stared into her dark eyes. "Because if she's not okay, *I'm* not okay."

A tear slid down the older woman's face, and he reached out and wiped it away with his thumb. "That's exactly what I needed to hear. I'm getting old, and I worry about her."

"I'll take care of her, Mama Lil," he admitted, hoping that this wasn't one of those "last" conversations.

Mama Lil was sick, but from what Ryleigh had told him, the cancer was treatable. And he'd been there earlier when the doctor had paid them a visit and reiterated that the prognosis was good. He wanted to ask her why she felt the need to say these things to him, but held his peace. Obviously, the older woman needed to get it out, and he wanted to make sure she knew he could be trusted.

"You better," she warned.

"I want to spend the rest of my life erasing her bad memories and replacing them with good ones."

Mama Lil reached a shaky hand out and caressed his face. "You love her, and she can feel it. I can see it in her eyes, hear it in her voice. There's a peace surrounding her. For the first time, she didn't balk at coming home. Ryleigh had a rough time of it, but she managed to make something of herself in spite of everything that has happened to her. That takes a lot of strength. I'm so proud of her. And it's because of that struggle that she'll try to push you away. I expect you won't let her."

"Hell no, I won't."

Mama Lil managed a soft laugh then. "I believe you. You have to be something special if she loves you, which she does. And because of that, I love you. So, if you're going to ask for my blessing to marry my girl, you got it."

Martin smiled. "How did you know?"

"I'm old, and there's nothing new under the sun. I can read you better than you can read that small ass computer screen."

He barked out a laugh. Ryleigh shifted in her chair, but didn't wake up. "I bet you can."

Standing up, he placed a kiss to the older woman's brow. "Thank you for trusting me your Ry-girl. I won't disappoint you. I promise."

Mama Lil smiled, and closed her eyes. "Now if you can promise to introduce me to a nice older gentleman, that would make this day even better."

Martin chuckled as Mama Lil drifted off the sleep.

"What are you laughing at?" Ryleigh stretched and opened her arms. He walked over to her and pulled her into a tight hug. "Mama Lil is hilarious."

"She woke up?"

"Yes, she did."

"That's good to hear. I'm so happy you're here with me."

Nudging her over, he sat down in the chair and pulled her onto his lap. "I'd never be anywhere else. I'm always going to be here for you."

Ryleigh wrapped her arms around his waist. "I believe you."

"Good. Because I meant what I said. You're going to be Mrs. Sullivan before long. No sense in hiding my intentions."

Giggling, Ryleigh peered up at him. "Well, in that case, I'd like to put in my request for forever."

Martin kissed her then, smiling against her lips as she sighed. "That can definitely be arranged."

EPILOGUE

5 *months after The Pact*

Ryleigh stared at her wedding ring. It was white gold, offset by sapphires and sandwiched between two white gold and sapphire bands. It was beautiful. Martin did good. Excellent. She couldn't believe she was actually married, and happy.

It seemed like it had taken them forever to get there. Even though he'd already made his intentions known, they'd tabled any discussion of a wedding because he'd been busy with his company and she'd been flying back and forth from Detroit to Rosewood Heights to take care of Mama Lil.

For Christmas, he'd surprised her with tickets to Punta Cana so they could be alone, but that didn't work out as planned because Mac announced her wedding. Martin hadn't understood why Ryleigh couldn't still go with him since the wedding was the week after their planned trip, but she'd explained that she had to be available for her bestie.

It had taken good head and a promise to learn how to pole dance to make it up to him, especially since it was a non-refundable ticket. Surprisingly, it had worked out for the best because she'd ended up being a natural on the pole. Martin had been so turned on when she rented a private dance studio that he'd gifted her with an unforgettable night of back-to-back orgasms.

After wedding mania had died down, and Mac and Alex were in wedded bliss, Martin had arranged for a first-class flight to Maui, and a suite full of gifts when they'd arrived at the five-star resort. When she'd protested, he'd shushed her, telling her that it was because she didn't ask for anything that he wanted to give her everything. He'd spoiled her, and she'd loved every minute of it.

A few days later, Martin had surprised her again when Mama Lil joined them on the island. The oncologist had cleared her for the flight and the vacation. His parents and his Granny had accompanied Mama Lil on the flight.

During a private dinner on the beach, he'd officially proposed with his final gift—the beautiful wedding ring she was wearing and never wanted to take off. Of course, Ryleigh had happily accepted. But she'd nearly fainted when he'd suggested they get married that week.

Martin, with the help of his mother, Mama Lil, and Events Coordinator at the resort, had arranged everything. They had a quick ceremony under the stars. The only sounds were the waves hitting the shore and them reciting the traditional marriage vows in front of his parents and her "Mama."

Since then, they'd been holed up in their room, wrapped around each other. She sighed, and glanced over at her fine-as-hell husband. He skin looked like it had been kissed by the sun. Brushing her hand over his bare chest and over the muscular lines of his stomach, she winked at him. He'd worn her out, but she wouldn't trade this feeling for the world.

Martin grabbed her hand and brought it up to his mouth, kissing her palm. "Ready?"

She grinned. He handed over her cell phone and she sent out the text. Within minutes, Ava called. *Always the first one.*

"Are you okay? How's Mama Lil?" Her friend was breathing hard, like she'd been running.

"I'm fine, Ava. What are you doing?"

"What do you mean?"

"You seem out of breath." Martin leaned in and placed a kiss on her shoulder. "Are you okay?"

"Sure. You texted emergency. You do realize it's ten o'clock at night."

It was only four o'clock in Hawaii, the day after they'd got married. "Fine. Let's do this."

They conferenced in the other ladies. As usual, her friends were all over the place, talking to each other and catching up quickly. This time, though, she needed to put the conversation to a halt.

Clearing her throat, she waited for the convo to die down. "I called you all for a reason."

"What the hell is it?" Raven asked.

"Right. It's late," Quinn added. "Is everything okay with Mama Lil?"

"Yes, she's fine. Enjoying the sun and the beach."

"You're one lucky something," Mac said. "Thank your lucky stars you're not in Detroit. Big snow storm coming. That Martin is spoiling you."

"So, listen," Ryleigh said. "I have news."

"Ry, just say it," Ava said, still sounding out of breath.

"What the hell are you doing, Ava?" Ryleigh pushed the mute button and looked at Martin. "I think she's doing it," she told him.

Martin laughed and dropped his head on her lap.

Unmuting the call, and placing them on speakerphone, she was just in time for Mac to suggest the same thing. They all burst out laughing.

Martin gave her a quick kiss before he scooted out of the bed and headed to the bathroom. A few seconds later, she heard running water.

"Okay, seriously." Ry figured she'd better steer the conversation back to the matter at hand, so she could join Martin in the bathtub. "I got married."

"To Martin with the very impressive—?"

"Shut up, Mac," Ryleigh ordered, glancing at the bathroom

door out of the corner of her eye, hoping he didn't hear that. "Yes, of course I married Martin. We did it last night, and I wanted to let you all know."

"I would have liked to be there," Quinn said.

She smiled at Martin as he climbed back on the bed. "I know, but it was the right time for us. His parents were here, and Mama Lil was here, so we just did it." They all gave their congratulations, before Ryleigh announced, "Martin is here."

Her friends all said a collective, "Hi, Marty-Mar."

Ryleigh laughed and Martin shot her a side-eye. "Ha ha, ladies," he said.

"I'm glad you made it official, Martin," Ava said. "Owen says congratulations."

"Thanks, man," Martin said.

"Okay, ladies, I have to cut it short." Ryleigh kissed Martin soundly. "We have things to do. Love you!"

Seconds later, she tossed her phone back in her bag. Martin crawled on top of her, settling between her legs. "You have on too many clothes," he said, kissing her nose then her lips.

"I know. Why don't you help me out?"

"We have a bath to enjoy, and I plan on letting you have your way with me again." He pulled his linen shirt off of her. "So, tell me about this impressive dick I have."

Ryleigh froze. "Oh no. You weren't supposed to hear that."

He laughed. "I'm fine with you thinking that, though."

Pinching him, Ryleigh giggled. "Be quiet."

"I love you, Ryleigh. I'll love you beyond forever."

She kissed him, tasting the sweetness of the sangria he'd had earlier at her request. The thought of them loving each other forever sounded perfect to her. "I'm looking forward to forever. I love you, too."

Dear Reader,

Thank you for taking this journey with me. I hope you enjoyed reading! Ryleigh and Martin captured my heart from the moment they laid eyes on each other during Ava's wedding reception.

If you're wondering what happened to Carter (Martin's best friend, and partner), I'll tell his story in my Spring release, Touched by You. And let me tell you… Carter will find his *one*, and "Brooklyn" is a trip.

Next up, is the first book in my Jackson's of Ann Arbor series, It's Always Been You. I've included the first chapter for you to preview. I hope you'll love it.

Make sure you pick up the other books in the Once Upon a Bridesmaid series and read all about how Mac, Raven, and Quinn handle *The Pact*.

Thank you so much for your support! And thank you for being #TeamElle! I truly appreciate you.

Love,

Elle

Yours Forever (Once Upon a Bridesmaid, Book 1) by Sherelle Green

Mackenzie "Mac" Cannon likes her men the same way she likes her coffee. Strong, black, and flavorful. However, while most women were trying to drink the entire coffee pot, Mac was more of a Keurig kind of girl, opting to have frivolous casual flings as opposed to meaningful relationships. While attending one of her best friends' weddings—in a moment influenced by too many mojitos—the Feng-Shui consultant foolishly agrees to a pact; to marry within the next year. Her friends don't think she's going to go through with it. Honestly, Mac is uneasy about the entire idea. But she doesn't mind cuddling up with the most mouth-watering cup of coffee she sees in the meantime... the best man, Alexander Carter.

Alex is successful, talented, devastatingly handsome, and surprisingly celibate. At least, he was, until a beautiful bombshell rocked his world before leaving him with nothing more than a piece of paper with a kiss on it in her wake. It's not that the CEO of an environmental engineer firm minds being used, but typically, if a woman wants him for only sex, he at least takes her to dinner first. Imagine his surprise when that same feisty vixen is placed into his life again, and as expected, she seems to be wearing her running shoes. Yet, this time, Alex is ready for the temptress. A little fun and games never hurt anyone, right? Unless fun and games starts looking a whole lot like promises and forever.

Embracing Forever (Once Upon a Bridesmaid, Book 3) by Sheryl Lister

After a string of failed relationships, and with three months left on the marriage pact she foolishly agreed to, Raven Holloway has just about given up on love. To take the sting out of her latest heartbreak, she does what she's always done—seek consolation in the arms of her best friend, Bryson Montgomery. Only this time, comfort turns to white-hot pleasure and a night she can't seem to forget. But the strong-willed physical therapist doesn't want to ruin a friendship and isn't ready to trust her heart again.

Marriage is definitely not on Bryson's radar. He has his hands full running his teen community center. Yet, he isn't prepared for the passion Raven unleashes in him and now he wants more. Raven is determined to keep him in the friend zone, but he's just as driven to show her how good they can be together. So, Bryson devises a seductive campaign to persuade Raven to embrace what he is offering…a love that will last forever.

Hopelessly Forever (Once Upon a Bridesmaid, Book 4) by Angela Seals

H opeless romantic. Never did two words describe anyone more than Quinn Jacobs...or at least in her mind. Quinn refuses to believe that her fun-loving idealist ways and sentimental dreamer mentality can be mistaken for a creepy class A clinger. When she makes a bet with her best friends from high school that she'll be married within a year, her delusional skewed view makes her think the task seems simple enough. After, repeatedly misinterpreting her romantic partner's affection for her, Quinn begins to think that maybe it isn't 'them' after all. Maybe she's the problem. And never has a person agreed with her more than the edgy and mysterious Paxton. They may be oil and water but if he can help her find a guy and accomplish her year-end goal, then who cares. But she slowly realizes that her whimsical ways may have agreed her to a world with Pax that she hadn't bargain for!

Paxton Wolfe prides himself on "keeping it real." Growing up in Orange Mound, Tennessee, taught him that if you want anything in life you had to work for it. When he starts his own flooring business, he kindly kissed away his thuggish lifestyle and entered the world of entrepreneurship. Women, money and full control are the perfect combination. Romance is just an unnecessary distraction and the last thing Pax is looking for. However; he hadn't planned for the bubbly, outgoing and clueless Quinn Jacobs to walk into his life. He's prepared to put in the work to help her land her dream man, but the one thing he didn't count on is the slow burning affection he starts to feel for the neurotic – yet mesmerizing – woman. Her uncontrollable honesty, endearing cuteness and inability to not wear her heart on her sleeve, makes her the most dangerous woman to fall for. But he's not in danger of that... right?

Chapter 1

Dr. Lovely Washington frowned when she felt the sun beaming down on her. Morning already? She patted the mattress, pausing when she felt cool skin under her palm. Drake. She pinched him. He pushed her hand away, grumbling something incoherent.

She smacked him. "Drake, what are you doing in my bed? And please...close the blinds. The light is killing me."

"Whashuleafmelone," he mumbled.

"I won't leave you alone until you get up and shut out the sun," she said, pinching her forehead. "My head hurts. And aren't you late or something?"

When he didn't move, she went to throw the sheet off, then stopped abruptly. Frowning, she patted her bare breasts. Uh-oh. *Where is my shirt?* Reluctantly, she slipped her hand under the sheet, over her stomach, her belly button, her--

She sat up abruptly. "Oh, my God, I'm naked!" Her mind raced to remember how she'd ended up like that. Last night was a blur. They'd booked a two-bedroom suite at the Bellagio because her family reunion was there. Two rooms, two beds. Yet Drake was in her bed and she was naked. "Oh no."

Drake had agreed to come because she hated going to these things by herself, and she wasn't particularly thrilled to face her family alone after her breakup with Derrick. When she needed someone—and she did—Drake was always there. He was her very best friend, since the age of two.

Her night had taken a turn for the worse when she'd received a call from the hospital that she'd lost a patient. Drake had dragged her out onto the strip to distract her. That was all she remembered.

She held her face in her hands, praying the shooting pain in her head would stop. She remembered something else. Tequila. Lots of it. Peeking through her fingers at Drake, she sucked in a deep breath. She couldn't tell if he was naked. He was lying on his stomach, his bare back gleaming at her in the sunlight. The sheet was draped low. Gently, she lifted the thin material.

"Drake!" she screeched, digging her nails into his back.

He pushed himself up on his elbows. "Ouch! What?"

"Get up," she ordered through clenched teeth. "Now."

He blinked and glanced at her with one eye. "What happened?"

Pulling the sheet with her, she hopped out of the bed. "Look at you," she said, pointing at his bare ass. "You're naked! Oh, my God."

"Oh, shit." He rolled out of bed onto the floor with a loud thump. Reaching up, he pulled the balled-up comforter with him. He finally stood up with the thick cover wrapped around his waist.

There was no movement—just eyes on eyes, heavy breathing and loud thoughts.

"Why are you naked?" Her heart raced as she watched his gaze drop to the bed.

Drake ran a hand through his wavy hair. "Why are *you* naked?"

She swallowed past a lump that had suddenly formed in her throat. "I asked you first," she croaked.

"Obviously, I don't know." He rolled his eyes and pinched the bridge of his nose.

"Why are you nervous?" she hissed. Drake was normally a calm and collected person, but they'd been friends long enough that she could recognize when he was nervous. After all, they'd been best friends for almost their whole lives.

His bloodshot eyes flashed to hers and his forehead creased. "I can't remember. I just remember walking on the strip doing shots."

"What do you mean you can't remember anything? You're naked!" she shrieked.

He pressed a hand to his temple. "Love, please, be quiet. You're making my head hurt worse. I don't need continuous updates on our lack of clothing."

She clutched the sheet to her chest. Tears pricked her eyes. "Drake, did we…?"

He held a hand up. "Don't say it. There has to be a good explanation."

"But we're both…" She dashed a tear off her cheek.

"Don't cry. That's how we got into this situation in the first place."

Placing her hands on her hips, she hissed, "What the hell is that supposed to mean?"

He covered his eyes. "Pull the sheet back up, Love."

Realizing she'd let it fall to the floor, she screamed and scrambled to pick it up, twisting the fabric around her body. "This can't be happening."

He motioned toward the bathroom. "Put some clothes on, for Christ's sake. This is already bad enough."

"Don't tell me what to do."

"Go in the bathroom," he demanded.

"You go in the bathroom," she countered, clutching the sheet in her palms.

"Love."

"What?"

He stalked toward her and she retreated until the back of her knees hit a chair. Overcorrecting, she stumbled into the seat.

Drake held out a hand and she took it and let him pull her to her feet. Then she shoved him away. "Get away from me, you ass."

He nudged her toward the en suite bathroom. "Look, get dressed. We're never going to figure this out standing here like this."

"I hate you," she growled as she stomped into the bathroom. Kicking the door closed, she leaned against it. A hotel robe was hanging on a hook and she snatched it and slipped it on. Once she secured the tie, she whipped the door open and stormed back into the bedroom toward a now clothed Drake.

His back was to her and he was murmuring curses to himself. She jumped on his back and wrapped an arm around his neck.

"You took advantage of me." With her other hand, she yanked his hair.

He fumbled with her weight and they both crashed down on the mattress. She flailed her arms and kicked at him until he grabbed her wrists and pinned them to the bed.

"Calm down," he pleaded. "Stop trying to fight me." The vein on the side of his temple jumped and his biceps bunched as he held her arms above her head.

Love was angry, but she was something else, too. Something that she'd never felt before. Well, tried to never feel before. His hard chest pressed against her soft one made it kind of difficult not to feel aroused.

"Get off of me, Drake." Needing to put some distance between them—because the last thing she needed was to be aroused—she bucked against him.

"Love, would you just…" He sighed, his hooded bedroom eyes boring into hers. *Bedroom eyes?* Her stomach fluttered and a warmth spread over her. She cursed her body for responding in ways she wouldn't dare admit.

Is he doing this on purpose? His eyes stayed on hers, seeming to look straight into her soul. Maybe he wasn't *trying* to turn her on, but he was.

"Promise me." His husky voice seemed to light a fire in her belly. "If I let you go you have to keep your hands to yourself."

"You took advantage of me," she muttered, her voice shaky. The anger she felt was melting under his gaze. Unclenching her fists, she let the tension ooze out of her arms. She chewed on her bottom lip. His breath fanned across her mouth and she couldn't help but entertain the idea of *letting* him take advantage of her.

"We don't know that," he said, snapping her out of her thoughts. "Neither of us remembers last night. You can't say for sure that we did anything but sleep."

"But we were naked," she murmured. *Why am I whispering?*

He squeezed her wrists. "Stop saying that. Let's concentrate on the present."

"Well, get your *naked* chest off of me and I'll try."

He jumped up, leaving her splayed across the bed, angry with her body for betraying her and with her mind for its wayward thoughts. She glared at the textured ceiling and prayed for a time machine that could zap her into yesterday, where Drake was merely annoying—not annoyingly sexy. Would she ever be able to look at him as the friend he was without thinking about his mussed hair and lean physique? Let alone the fine line of hair that trailed down his stomach and disappeared under the waistband of the low-riding sweatpants he'd donned. She tightened the belt on the robe and sat up, smoothing her hair back.

"What *do* you remember?" he asked, in the tone he often used on his patients. Detached.

Obviously, he wasn't as affected as she was. *Ouch.* She cleared her throat. "Lana called. One of my patients went into labor and was admitted to the hospital, possible peripartum cardiomyopathy," she answered, as if she was reporting to her chief resident during rounds. "Instead of paging me, she had paged Blake. The mother insisted on a natural birth, but her heart couldn't take the labor. She died. I was upset that I wasn't there, so you took me out to get my mind off of it."

He lifted his eyes toward the ceiling and muttered a string of curses. "I keep replaying last night over and over in my head. I can't remember how we got in bed. I remember the bar, the shots. You were finally loosening up. When we left Caesars, you were tipsy, so I had to kind of hold on to you. I can see us laughing at random people on the way back to the room. Then we ran into a few of our high school classmates. They asked us to go out with them, but you didn't want to, so we headed back here. Then..." He averted his gaze, swallowed roughly.

She bowed her head and wondered what he'd just remembered. They were friends. Best friends, in fact. They'd grown up finishing each other's sentences. Love knew all of Drakes "tells" and was certain he'd just filled in some blanks.

"The bar and walk I remember," she croaked. "That's about it."

It wasn't a complete lie. She'd been very inebriated, inconsolable over the loss of her patient. Drake had done what he always did—make it better, help her forget.

"Hopefully, it'll come back to us later. For now, we can't assume anything happened."

They'd shared the same bed many times during their lifelong friendship, and nothing had ever happened. Not even an accidental brush of arms. Hell, he'd seen her in her underwear plenty of times. But…

"We were still clearly on our own sides of the bed," he continued, without meeting her gaze. "There's no clue—"

"I feel sore," she blurted out. "My whole body does."

"You were drunk. You could've fallen or something."

Love wondered when Drake had turned into Mr. Positivity. The proof was staring them right in the face. The bed. She scanned the rest of the room before zeroing in on the bed again. Frowning, she walked closer to it and ran a finger over the tiny bright red spot. Closing her eyes, she gasped. "Oh, my God!"

"Stop saying that," he said, between clenched teeth.

"It's blood. There's your clue. We had sex."

"Love, you're not a virgin. The blood is probably from a paper cut or something."

"You don't really believe that, do you?"

He glared at her. "Just…be quiet. Let me think."

"You know we had sex," she muttered under her breath. And the worst part? She didn't remember the details. If she was going to participate in something that would more than likely ruin her friendship with Drake, she would've liked to remember it.

THE FORBIDDEN MAN Excerpt

Chapter 1

"Don't move."

Sydney Williams glanced at her watch. "Allina, I have to go. I'm meeting Den in thirty minutes." In a few short months, Syd was finally going to marry her longtime love, Caden Smith, affectionately known as Den.

Sydney flinched when she received a playful whack on the behind.

"I told you to be still. I'm almost finished. There. You can turn around."

Sydney sucked in a deep breath then turned and looked at her reflection. The white silk, floor-length gown fit her perfectly. Smoothing a hand over her hip, she eyed the tiny crystals adorning the plunging neckline. It was simple, understated—exactly how she wanted it.

"What do you think?" Allina said, biting her thumbnail as she stepped back. "I think it looks much better with your hair up."

"It's beautiful. Den's going to love it." Sydney ignored the look her friend gave her and the quick rolling of her brown eyes. Sighing, she took one last glance at herself, turned around, and raised her arms. Allina unzipped her and she rushed into the fitting room. "I appreciate this, girlfriend. You're truly gifted," she told her from behind the curtain.

Tossing the gown over the door for her friend, she dressed. When she was finished, she slipped into her sandals and pulled the curtain open. Allina was zipping up the garment bag.

"I'm ready to invest when you're ready to go out on your own," Sydney said, rummaging through her purse. "It's time."

"It'll be ready for you Friday after five o'clock," Allina said, changing the subject. She tucked a stray braid that had fallen out into her neat bun.

Before Sydney could go into the countless reasons why it was better for Allina to venture out and open her own boutique, her cell phone vibrated. Muttering a curse, she shook her bag and felt around for the cell phone. Sighing heavily, she grabbed a hold of it and pulled it out. After a quick glance at the anonymous number, she was tempted to ignore the call—except she was planning a wedding and it could be someone calling to confirm something.

Grumbling a curse, she answered, "This is Sydney."

"I wasn't sure you'd answer." The nasal-toned voice of her fiancé's ex-booty call, Laney, immediately put Sydney in a bad mood.

"Can't make the right choice all the time. Why the hell are you calling me?" Syd snapped.

"I just thought you'd want to know—"

"And how did you get my number?" She dropped her purse on the chair.

Curiosity prevented her from hanging up on the other woman. It was no secret she couldn't stand Laney, but she couldn't help but wonder why she was calling her. "Look, I'm doing you a favor," Laney said. "The least you can do is treat me with some respect."

Syd's interest turned to dread at Laney's snide tone. The last "favor" from Laney had almost destroyed her relationship with Den. It took months to get over the fact that he'd cheated on her while she was away at graduate school. She gripped her phone. "Laney, what the hell do you want?"

Allina, who'd just returned from the back, stopped in her tracks at the mention of that name.

Placing a hand over the receiver, Syd mouthed to her friend, "I'm fine. Go ahead and finish what you were doing."

Allina didn't look convinced, but walked away anyway, glancing back as she headed toward the counter.

"I'll just cut to the chase," Laney sneered.

"Please do." Something told Syd to have a seat, but she remained on her feet. Although the other woman couldn't see her, she didn't want to give even the slightest impression that she was affected by anything Laney had to say. "I don't have all day."

"If you think you're going to be happy with Den, you're fooling yourself."

"What do you know about it?" Sydney asked with a snicker.

"Everything. I know that Den has been lying to you for months. He told you that you could trust him. That he'd never hurt you again. That he wanted to start fresh, confess everything...the random woman at a bar story...then he realized that he couldn't live without you...couldn't wait to make you his wife."

Syd felt sick to her stomach as Laney droned on. The fact that this woman knew all of her business wasn't the worst part. It was what she feared was coming next that was giving her fits.

"Sydney, did you hear me?" Laney called through the receiver.

She swallowed, then cleared her throat. "Just say what you need to say and stop wasting my time with this shit, Laney."

"And I'll bet you believed him, too." Laney laughed, and the sound made Syd's skin crawl. "The thing is, he may be ready to make you his wife, but he surely can't keep that promise of never hurting you again, because *I* was the woman at the bar and it definitely wasn't a random hook-up. We've been seeing each other for months now—at your house, in your bed."

Closing her eyes, Syd barely flinched when the phone landed on her toes, then the carpeted floor, with a thump.

Allina rushed over to her. "What's going on?"

"Oh God," Syd cried. "This can't be happening."

She vaguely felt Allina nudging her, heard her begging her to say something, anything. It seemed like everything was happening in slow motion. Over the last eight months, she'd spent thousands on the details, the plans, the invitations... Oh God, her family was coming. They'd purchased tickets and paid for hotel rooms. What would they think of her? How would she face them?

"Sydney!" Allina yelled, shaking her out of her thoughts. "What's wrong?"

Syd wouldn't bother calling Den to confirm Laney's story. In her heart, she knew the other woman was telling the truth. She was sure it had happened just the way Laney described. And it wasn't because Laney was such a truth teller. It was only because Den had lied to her more times than she cared to admit, more times than she ever told anyone. He'd promised her he was a changed man, but she knew change didn't come easy to Den. She wanted to drive to his job and embarrass him in front of his employees, demand that he explain himself, order him to do something—anything—to make this seem less real, less devastating. Would there be anything he could say to justify this? Wasn't it her fault for believing the lies, taking him back, and choosing to never hold him accountable every single time he'd hurt her? Yet, even as her heart seemed to split open and the pain crept into her bones, she couldn't muster up any blame for the man that she loved. No, there was no one to blame but herself.

Blinking, Sydney zeroed in on her phone lying on the floor and picked it up. She didn't bother checking to see if Laney was still on the line. She turned it off and tossed it into her purse.

What the hell am I going to do now?

"Do me a favor?" she asked Allina, grabbing her keys and heading toward the door. "Call Calisa. Tell her to cancel…everything."

"Wait," Allina called to her before she opened the door. "Don't just leave like this. Something happened. You're upset and crying. You can't drive like this." She walked over and took Sydney's purse from her hand. "Come on. I'm closing up. Keep me company?"

Sydney wiped her eyes angrily then plopped down on an empty chair. "Allina, I know you have an event this evening. You don't have to stay with me."

"I have a few hours." Allina sat down next to her and squeezed her hand. "I'm here for whatever you need, okay?"

"I need a drink." She pulled some tissue from a dispenser and blew her nose.

"I have some wine in the back," Allina offered. "We keep it for bridal parties."

"Bring it out and let me wallow."

"Syd, what happened?" her friend asked again, concern in her brown eyes. She ran her hand over Syd's back.

"He cheated on me," Syd said on a sigh. "Again. With her. Again."

Allina shook her head, disgust playing on her features. "That fucking...piece of shit."

Syd knew that her friend didn't care for Den. It'd been painfully obvious for months. Hell, it'd been years since she'd heard Allina curse, and she'd said "fucking" and "shit" in the same sentence. But Lina wasn't the type to voice her opinion about someone else's relationship. Never had been. She'd always supported Sydney's decisions even if she didn't agree with them.

"You don't have to say it, Lina. I already know you hate him."

Allina sighed heavily, but continued to focus on the end-of-the-night receipts.

The silence from her friend did nothing but heighten her anxiety, and she realized she wanted—no; needed—to hear her thoughts. Exasperated, she told her, "Fine. Say it."

"What's there to say?" Allina shrugged. "He's an ass, but you already knew that."

Ouch. Allina always did have a way of making things very plain. So plain it irked the hell out of her.

"He hurt you again," Allina continued. "I can't say I'm surprised, but I do think it's better that you found out now instead of after you married him."

Syd grabbed hold of Allina's wrist. "Please don't say anything, not even to Kent," Syd begged.

Syd had tried to play matchmaker for Allina and Den's brother Kent for years. But the stubborn duo had refused to see the potential in one another that she had. Instead of dating, they were firmly in the "we're just good friends" camp.

"I never do," Allina smiled slightly and patted her hand.

Releasing her hold, Syd stood up and pulled on her shirt. "Where the hell is that wine?"

Allina disappeared into the back of the store and emerged a

few minutes later with a bottle of Red Moscato, Syd's favorite. Pouring it into a cup, she held it out to her.

Instead of taking the cup Syd grabbed the bottle, and put it to her lips.

"Allina?" Syd belched and muttered, "Excuse me."

"Yeah?"

"What am I going to do?" Syd felt like she was going to choke on her tears. It was hard to even think straight. She had no clue where to start. "How am I going to tell everyone? My dad, Red..." Gulping down more of the wine, she covered her mouth when another burp escaped. "Oh God, Red is going to kill him."

Syd knew her twin brother Jared, or Red as they called him, wasn't Den's biggest fan. He'd always felt that Den didn't appreciate her and took her for granted. Every chance he got, he told her that Den didn't deserve her loyalty.

"Red is going to be fine, Syd. He's an attorney. He knows how to keep his cool."

"It's really my fault," she confessed. "I shouldn't have taken him back again. I knew he wasn't ready. When he proposed, I knew it wasn't right. He did it during my lunch hour, for Christ's sake. Who does that?"

The quick, unromantic proposal had been the talk for weeks within their small circle of friends. Even Den's brothers thought the approach was rather trifling and had told him so countless times. Syd, on the other hand, made excuses for Den: it was romantic to her, they hadn't been able to schedule a dinner, or it was always her dream to get proposed to in an ordinary way. That last excuse was kind of true. She did envision a proposal during a random weeknight dinner or during their favorite television show. Sitting in the drive-through at Mickey D's? Yeah, somehow that didn't make the cut, but she was happy and couldn't wait to become Den's wife.

Allina scratched her head and peered up at the ceiling.

"Allina, I know you have something to say. You always hold back. It's the reason why you never told Kent that you have feelings for him that go beyond just friends, or why you don't have your own shop. You're a kick-ass seamstress, with a good business sense. But you never speak your mind, say how you really feel about stuff."

"Maybe it's not my place," Allina said, her pale cheeks now a dark shade of crimson. "And you promised never to say anything out loud about Kent and my true feelings for him."

Syd smiled. "I'm sorry. I did promise, didn't I? Kent would be lucky to have your tall ass on his arm. You're so beautiful. Just wish you'd realize it." When Allina didn't respond, Syd finished off the bottle and set it on a table nearby. Her friend was modest as this day from hell was long, so it was no use ever paying her a compliment. "You have another one of these?" she asked after a few minutes of silence.

Allina glanced at her before heading to the back. Syd couldn't be sure, but she swore she saw it on Allina's face...pity. Her friend thought she was pitiful. Maybe she was.

When Allina returned, Syd reached out to grab the bottle. But Allina held it back. "Syd, maybe you should slow down. You still have to drive."

"I'll slow down when you tell me what you're really thinking."

Sighing heavily, Allina sat down. "Okay. I just think you deserve better. Den is okay, charming, funny, and attentive when he wants to be. I don't think any of us doubts that he loves you. But love and respect are two different things and one or the other isn't enough to sustain a relationship on its own. He's hurt you so much.... Sometimes it's better to let it go than to keep trying when a relationship isn't working."

"I love him." Her words sounded hollow even to Syd's own ears. Allina hadn't told her anything that she hadn't already thought herself over the past few months.

"I know you do, sweetie. But Den has issues. You said yourself that sometimes you feel like you can't even leave him alone because you're so worried he won't take his meds, or he won't make it without you. In the meantime, it's like you're willing to accept everything he throws at you."

Den's bipolar disorder had wreaked havoc in the lives of those closest to him, especially her and his other brother, Morgan. He had a habit of not taking his meds when he was busy. A part of him always wanted to test the limits, see if he could do without the Lithium.

"You don't understand," Syd told her. "He needs me. And I owe him."

"You don't, Syd." Tears gathered in Allina's eyes and she turned away to wipe them. "I just wish you'd realize that and maybe take this as an opportunity to start fresh."

"Start where?" Syd dropped her gaze to the floor. "I've been with him so long I don't even remember life without him."

"But you've also sacrificed so much for him and the relationship. You've made excuses for his behavior, blamed everything on his disease. What if he's just being himself? Ask yourself why he cheated on you with her in the first place."

Syd had asked herself that question so many times. "I wasn't here. I moved out of the state. How could I expect him to be faithful when I wasn't sure I was coming back?" It was the blanket answer she'd repeated to herself so often she believed it.

"You moved to go to graduate school," Allina said, obviously not accepting the bland excuse. "You went to help your sick father."

"Still, we didn't make any promises when I left," she insisted, even as she realized her defense of Den was more out of habit. The fact was, Den hadn't proven himself worthy of her loyalty in a long time. Just like her brother said.

"Well, you're back now." Allina picked up a safety pin off the floor and tossed a used tissue into a small waste bin. "It's been years and it seems that you're in this perpetual state of cleaning up behind him."

There it was again. The cold, hard truth. And she couldn't deny it any longer.

"He made a promise when he proposed to you, Syd," Allina continued. "He broke it. You have to decide if you're going to keep accepting that, because you know he's not going to take responsibility for his actions. It's always someone else's fault."

Allina was right. She had given Den more than enough chances and she was tired. The relationship was beyond repair at this point. And even if it wasn't, she wasn't sure she'd want to fix it. As much as she loved him, she had to face the fact that it just wasn't going to work, and he wasn't healthy for her. The wedding was off.

Morgan tapped on the door to the small storefront, then pressed the bell. He'd rushed over when he'd received Allina's call begging him to come and pick Syd up. She'd spouted something about heartbreak, wine, and weddings, so he dropped everything and raced there. As he waited, he wondered what he'd find when the door opened.

Allina opened the door. "I'm so glad you came."

"What's going on?" he asked, ducking under the low-hanging bell and stepping into the shop. He heard the radio blasting Destiny's Child and what sounded like...singing, loud and off-key.

"I tried to take the bottle away from her, but she's in a mood," Allina told him. "I would stay but I have an event. I tried to call Red, but he's not answering. Calisa didn't pick up either. I even tried Kent. So you're it."

"Where the hell is Den?" Morgan muttered, shaking his head and running a hand over his face. He cringed when Syd hit an awkward high note. "You still haven't told me what's going on, Allina."

She sighed. "That's...not an option. I'm sorry if I interrupted your evening, but I didn't know who else to call. I'd tell you what happened, but I promised I wouldn't."

He muttered a curse under his breath. "Where is she?"

"Back there," she answered, pointing to one of the private bridal rooms in the rear of the store.

Morgan followed her toward the music. Although Allina hadn't technically spilled the beans, he'd already guessed that his brother was the reason Syd was belting out through-with-love songs at the top of her lungs. Obviously, Syd was in no condition to drive. And he wanted to throttle his older brother for undoubtedly breaking her heart. Again.

Rounding the corner, he stopped at the sight of Syd sprawled out on the couch singing Dru Hill's "In My Bed."

"Oh, shit," Morgan grumbled.

"Tell me about it," Allina mumbled under her breath. She stood over Syd and nudged her. "Hey. Morgan's here."

Syd's eyes widened. "Morgan? What is he...?" She pointed at him accusingly. "What are *you* doing here?"

"Syd," he said softly, approaching her. "What are you doing?"

"Singing," she said simply. "And drinking."

He bent down to Syd's level. Pushing a few stray curls out of her face, he took a good look at her, noting that her hazel eyes were bloodshot and her mocha skin had a pink flush to it. Sure signs that she was drunk. "Are you going to tell me what happened?"

"I don't know." Syd shrugged. "Can I trust you?"

He chuckled, amused by the question. "You know you can."

"I don't know." She traced his cheek with her fingers. "You're his brother. Did you know you had dimples just like him?"

He squeezed her hand and gently removed it from his face. "You can trust me."

"But you don't look like him," she said, her voice low and hoarse. "You have nice facial hair. And you're much taller and thinner. Between me and you," she whispered. "I think Den is going to get fat in a couple of years. He eats too much pizza."

"Tell me what happened," he said, trying to get her back on track.

"He cheated on me with that whore, Laney. Again," she slurred, picking at the mound of curls on the top of her head, pulled into what she often referred to as a bitchy bun. "He fucked me over. I mean, the first time I was away. I gave him that one because I lived in another state at the time. And even though she ended up pregnant... I still forgave his ass." She sobbed and dropped her empty paper cup on the floor.

Morgan remembered the drama surrounding Den's first affair with Laney. The woman had gotten pregnant and couldn't wait to tell the world. Den had refused to 'fess up even though they all told him to tell Syd before she found out from someone else, namely Laney. Eventually, Syd found out the truth when Laney followed her through the mall, taunting her with the sordid details of their ongoing relationship. Shortly after, though, Laney suffered a miscarriage.

Syd squeezed his arm, jarring him from his thoughts. "I forgave him again a week ago when he confessed that he'd slept with some random woman he met in a bar," she cried, her tears falling unchecked down her cheeks. "He said it happened months ago, before he proposed, when we were having that rough patch. But it was really last week. And then I find out it's *her*. He played me. And I let him. Again. She called me, ya know," she babbled on. "She wanted me to know that he fucked her in my bed. He couldn't even take her somewhere else."

"Son of..." Allina groaned. "You didn't tell me that earlier."

"I didn't want to say it out loud," Syd admitted quietly. "Allina already thinks I'm stupid for taking him back in the first place. You probably pity me, too."

"I don't, Syd," Allina said, her voice cracking. She dropped to her knees next to Morgan. "I'm here for you."

"You do," Syd told Allina. "You probably think I'm going to take him back again."

Morgan looked at Allina, who stared down at the floor. He guessed she really did believe Syd would take his cheating brother back. Probably because she always did. Sometimes it would take a few days, a few months, but she always took him back. He'd spent a lot of time trying to figure out why. In the end, he figured her reasons for making excuses for Den's behavior matched his own. He'd spent most of his life doing the same thing, years of ignoring the bad and concentrating on the good. In spite of all Den's flaws, they'd seen the man that protected those he loved with everything he had; the man that could make anyone laugh no matter the circumstance; the smart, talented businessman... a man worth saving.

Glancing back at Syd, anger coursed through him. The Den he wanted to save seemed lost to him. It had been a long time since he felt the need to make excuses for his brother, and that was partly because of Syd. Mostly it was because Morgan resented Den. He'd given up a lot for his brother, but ultimately had made the decision to pull away because he was tired of being pulled into Den's hell. This latest debacle was simply Den being Den—selfish, careless, and impulsive. And he hoped Syd was finished with him for good this time.

"Come on, babe," he said, picking Syd up and cradling her in his arms.

"Are you going to take her home?" Allina asked, her eyes filled with unshed tears. "I mean, are you taking her home with you?"

He nodded as he made his way through the store with Allina right on his heels. "I'll keep trying to reach Red," he told Allina. "In the meantime, I'll make sure she's taken care of. Thanks for calling me."

"Morgan? Her purse," Allina called. She hooked Syd's tote on his arm. "I was going to say tell Den to go screw himself, but just take care of my friend. I parked her car in the garage. It'll be good there overnight."

He nodded. "For what it's worth, I want to kick his ass, too."

BOOKS BY ELLE WRIGHT

Edge of Scandal Series

The Forbidden Man

His All Night

Her Kind of Man

All He Wants for Christmas

The Jacksons of Ann Arbor

It's Always Been You

Wherever You Are

Wellspring Series

Touched By You

ABOUT THE AUTHOR

There was never a time when **Elle Wright** wasn't about to start a book, wasn't already deep in a book—or had just finished one. She grew up believing in the importance of reading, and became a lover of all things romance when her mother gave her her first romance novel. She lives in Michigan.

Join the Elle Wright Reader Group!

Connect with Elle!

www.ellewright.com
info@ellewright.com

www.ingramcontent.com/pod-product-compliance
Lightning Source LLC
Chambersburg PA
CBHW060617130626
46555CB00002B/541